MW01593786

The Undying Ones

Revenants

Christina L Olson

The Undying Ones – Revenants (The Undying Ones #1)

Christina L Olson

ISBN-13: 978-1974370085

ISBN-10: 1974370089

To my beloved
Husband,

No, the Butler didn't do it.

Table of Contents

"The boundaries which divide Life from Death are at best shadowy and vague. Who shall say where the one ends, and where the other begins?"

~ Edgar Allen Poe

Chapter One

Mattie was the first to see her.

She had not planned on going to her father's workshop that day. It was well known that the Toymaker had a terrible temper - a temper that had only grown worse as the long years passed and the madness that afflicted them all eventually took hold - and he did not like anyone, not even his own daughter, prowling through his things. However, Mattie had broken her mask while scavenging for supplies around the castle and only the Toymaker had the resin that would hold the pieces together.

His workshop was an old barn that leaned heavily against the thick outer bailey wall. Light flickered through the gaping holes between the rotting boards, casting dim shadows that danced across the barren ground outside. Mattie watched for a moment, indecision threatening her resolve; was her father in there? If he was, would he even remember her if he saw her? Like his anger, his confusion had also increased over the years, and it made her chest ache when she saw him wandering the halls and he didn't recognize her. Maybe she should come back later, right before morning, when everyone was asleep...

She shook her head to clear her thoughts. No, she couldn't wait till later - she had to fix her mask or face the consequences if she was caught without it.

She forced herself to creep from shadow to shadow, moving slowly and painstakingly closer to the door. She had honed her skills over the years while playing with her friends in the decaying castle, and she knew she could be as quiet as a mouse, but she still found herself uttering a small prayer that her father would not hear her approach.

For a second time, her fear almost got the better of her, and she froze against the side of the barn. She didn't *really* need her mask. After all, the others went around without any masks on all the time, so why should she have to wear one? Her father was the only one that insisted she wear it constantly... or so Rordan and Talesin, her friends, told her. She assumed it was because he couldn't stand that his daughter was not as beautiful as the dolls he used to create. However, looks did not matter much anymore - they were all as ugly as the gargoyles guarding the castle walls.

She felt naked without the comforting weight of the mask on her face though, and so she pushed forward, edging along the weathered walls of the barn, pausing occasionally to look again and again for any movement inside. There was still no sign of any life inside the barn, and Mattie allowed herself to breathe a little easier. He was not here. No one was. She eased the doors open just wide enough to allow her to slip in.

Once upon a time, the Toymaker's workshop had been clean and organized, but that was before the bad times... before the plague and the curse. Now the inside of the workshop was cluttered, packed with discarded nick-knacks, furniture, and other bits and pieces of junk. A thick film of dust covered everything and cobwebs hung in the corners and stretched from the roof to various objects below.

She weaved around piles of broken spindles and shattered mirrors and then ducked under a fallen beam. Long shelves lined the back wall and she picked through the cluttered mess on them, pushing aside pots of paint, rusty scissors, and bits of thread in her search. This had been where he used to keep it - or so she thought she remembered - but the little jar was missing from the shelves.

She stared at them, chewing on a lip as she tried to think of where it might have gone to. Had someone assumed that it was food and eaten it? The resin was made from animal bones, sap, and eggs, among other things, so it *might* be edible. She couldn't imagine anyone wanting to eat it though as it stunk to high heaven. There was a chance that her father had moved it, but the thick layer of grime covering everything told her that that was unlikely. Maybe it had fallen off the shelf...

She crouched, searching the ground near the shelves and caught a glint of something smooth underneath the shelves. The resin! She dug the jar out, laid the pieces of her broken mask out on the ground, and, holding her breath against the fumes, she began to glue them together.

"Don't worry," Mattie whispered to it as she started to piece it back together. "You'll be back to normal in no time at all. And I swear I won't do anything so foolish ever again."

The mask was silent. Neither judging nor doubting her.

Rumor in the great hall that night was that the birds who used to nest in the cracks in the castle walls had finally returned. While the others plotted ways to catch the birds and add them to the communal stew,

Mattie had been far more excited about the prospect of fresh eggs. It had been years since she had tasted meat, but even longer since she'd had a fresh hard-boiled egg. After years of subsiding on nuts and berries that fell from the few trees able to cling to the mountain slope below the castle, and whatever odds and ends could be scrounged up to add to the sludge in the cauldron, the prospect of having a fresh egg or two made her mouth water and her stomach grumble.

Deciding that she would claim the eggs before anyone else could, Mattie ducked out of the Great Hall before anyone noticed and made her way to the collapsed outer wall. She clambered over it, following it around until the wall joined the sharp mountain side, peering up into the shadows for any signs of a bird's nest as she walked. She did not see one, but near the waterfall that thundered against the Northern edge of the castle, she did catch sight of a bird taking off from a cliff. Perhaps it was there?

The rocks and the wall by the waterfall were dangerous. They were often slippery from mist, and were covered in thick layers of algae. However, Mattie was small and quick and sure of hand and foot. Believing that there would be a nest where she'd seen the bird, she began to climb toward it.

She had been doing quite well until she was distracted by the lights behind the water cascading over the cliffside.

She stared at them, entranced. First, she glanced at the moon, thinking that they must reflect its light on the water. However, the light from the moon was bluish, and the lights in the waterfall were golden like candle lights – only much larger. But there was no space behind the waterfall for people to wander, and no way to get there if there was.

Mattie closed her eyes, thinking that perhaps she was just seeing things - but when she reopened them, the lights were still there, bobbing behind the curtain of water. She crept closer so she could investigate the source of the mystery, but slipped and fell while reaching for a crevasse to cling to. Thankfully she managed to catch herself from falling any further, but her mask had come loose and it shattered against the rocks beneath her.

When she looked for the lights again, they were gone. Torn between pursuing them or fixing her mask, she decided on the latter. Now, here she sat, gluing it back together.

"I'll be more careful next time." She promised the mask as she worked.

Once she finished, she sat back and surveyed her work while it dried. The results were not the prettiest - the resin oozed between the cracks in thick gray lines marring the white face - however it would do. "See? All fixed."

The mask was still silent.

She snorted to herself - and they called her father the crazy one. Even though he might not recognize where he was or the people around him most of the time, at least he didn't talk to inanimate objects as if he expected a response.

A sharp gust of wind shook the barn. It startled her, making her jump in surprise and almost drop her mask again. She grabbed it before it could crash to the ground and clutched it to her chest with a sigh of relief. The wind rattled the walls again, making the timbers shake and groan, and somewhere in the shadows she could hear the whisper of fabric. Had her father returned? She turned around, looking for the source. Thankfully the barn was still empty - but now she noticed heavy black curtains sectioning a corner off from the rest of the barn.

How very odd. Was her father working on something again? She didn't think he was still capable of building things! At some point during the chaos after the curse, his hands and fingers had been broken. Rordan said it was because the King's Guards had tortured him after the queen disappeared, because they thought he might know where she went. However, Talesin claimed it was because the Guards enjoyed torturing people, often pulling their victims out of their bed for no reason at all - which was how he and his brother had both gotten the scars on their face. Regardless of how her father had been injured though, his hands had never been set properly and became gnarled over time until he could barely use them.

He stopped working, and took to wandering the halls at night. Perhaps that was why his mind was so shattered; those who had something to do, like the guards, seemed to stay sane longer, while those who didn't, like her father, went mad and forgot themselves and their families.

But if he was building something again... Perhaps there was hope. Perhaps he wasn't quite as lost as everyone thought he was.

She knew she should run - the Toymaker could return at any moment - however she longed to see what was on the other side of the curtains. Would it be as pretty and majestic as that mechanical bird that he had made for the Queen? It had rusted over the years until it was frozen still, but she had heard stories of its former glory. Or would it be twisted like his poor hands?

Her curiosity finally won out over her common sense and she pushed the curtain open and stepped inside.

Mattie blinked, letting her eyes adjust to the brightness. The room beyond was like another world; it was spotless and bright compared to the chaos beyond the curtain. Someone had taken the time to sweep the stone floors clean of dirt and dust all the shelves. Lit candles sat on every available surface, their light magnified by the mirrors that hung on the walls and ceiling.

She quickly pulled on her mask, not wanting to see her wretched face reflected tenfold. She needn't worry though; all the mirrors were all angled towards a table that sat in the middle of the room. A blanket covered it, hiding something lumpy figure from sight. A hand stuck out from under the blanket. Its nails and fingertips were a dark purple, almost black, but the rest of its skin was as pale as her porcelain mask.

She frowned to herself. Her father made a doll? But why? There were no more children around to appreciate such a thing, and the Queen, who loved dolls and the Toymaker's other creations, was long gone. She disappeared ages ago, during the chaos that ensued after the castle had been cursed.

And where had he gotten the supplies to make such a thing anyways? They were trapped here without any way to escape: the villagers had blocked the gates with rubble and destroyed the bridge when they learned of what was going on in the castle. It was possible that he might have supplies left over from before hidden somewhere, but she doubted it. The King had demanded that his subjects turn in any supplies that might possibly sustain them once he learned of the Villager's treachery and anything that might be edible was confiscated by his men – including much of her father's supplies. Leather might not have much nourishment to it, but it could be boiled down into gruel. It tasted horrible, but it took the edge off the constant hunger in their bellies.

She ran a fingertip over the back of the hand; the hide was smooth to the touch. Even if her father had found a way to secret it away, such fine leather should have dried out and cracked long ago. She could feel something hard and narrow shift under the hide and gasped. He had even carved bones for this thing and strung them together with twine! She could feel them moving beneath her touch. Only, now that she thought about it, wooden bones and string weren't supposed to move like that, and even the softest leather from the youngest calves wasn't that soft. It felt like her own skin did, like her own hand.

She tucked her cloak tight about her arms in a useless attempt to fight off the chill that ran across her flesh. She was simply letting her imagination get away with her. That was it. The thing under the blanket was just a doll. An odd life-sized doll, but a doll nonetheless. She would uncover it and she would see that her fears were unfounded.

She took a breath to steady herself and pulled the blanket away.

She was wrong: it wasn't a doll, but the body of a dead woman lying on the table.

"It's not possible." Mattie murmured, staring at it in shock. "It can't be."

Denizens of the castle had been unable to die since the curse claimed them. Many had tried over the years. First, they jumped from the tallest towers in the castle, however, even though the fall damaged their bodies, their minds continued to live on. Then others tried starving themselves, but while they wasted away to nothing, their bodies never gave out. Regardless of what they did, or what happened to them, they would keep on living, on and on and on until the end of time.

So how did her father find a dead body?

Maybe she was finally going mad like her father and simply imagined the thing. Maybe the endless days and nights had finally broken her, like so many others. She had been talking to her mask earlier, after all. She closed her eyes, just like she did at the waterfall, but when she opened them again, the body was still there, and when she touched the body's hand again it was still solid beneath her fingertip.

She, whoever she had been before, was lovely. Copper hair crowned a delicate oval face that was free of any pock marks or scars. Her eyebrows were plucked into thin lines that arched over closed eyes. Her eyelashes, thick and dark, rested against her pale cheeks, and her full lips were painted a dark wine red. Perhaps she was a member of the nobility? Talesin, one of her only friends, had told her that they'd been the first to succumb to the curse, accepting it willingly because they thought it would save them from the plague. However, there were no pock marks or scars marking the flawless skin, only thick black stitching here and there across her torso.

If she wasn't one of them, then that meant that she was from the villages – only that wasn't possible either. While those trapped in the castle had eventually figured out ways over the walls, there was no way to cross the wide chasm that separated them from the rest of the world; the bridge that led from the old village to the castle had been destroyed during the bad years, the mountains the castle was built into were too steep to climb, and there was no way through the waterfall. Besides, a villager had not come near the old town and castle in over a hundred years.

There was a sound from behind her and Mattie turned to run, but a figure cloaked in black blocked the way.

Her father had returned to his workshop.

Once he had been tall, however his form had been twisted by the plague that ravaged their kingdom during the curse. Now he was hunched over and required the assistance of a cane to walk. His hair was matted and hung over his pockmarked face, but Mattie could see his blue eyes peering out at her from behind the dreadlocks. "Matryoshka? What are you doing here?"

"Nothing, Papa," She stammered, trying to think of something that might appease him. "I was just coming to check on you – I haven't seen you in the great hall for several nights now."

"Hm." He did not look as if he believed her, but then he had always been able to see through her lies. "I see you have introduced yourself to Marionette. How do you like her? Is she not beautiful?"

"Papa, what have you done?"

"I have created new life, like I did with you so very long ago."

"But, Papa, you didn't create me..."

"I laid with your mother, didn't I? At least that's what they tell me." The toymaker stopped and stared at her, his expression suddenly confused. "Who are you?"

"Your daughter, Mattie."

"Mattie?"

"Matryoshka. Remember?"

"Oh, yes, Matryoshka. I see you've met Marionette."

Mattie closed her eyes and counted to ten. "Yes, Papa. But who is she..."

"I do not know, they brought her to me." He stepped past her and bent over the body's hand and then face, leaning close to inspect his work. "She was broken and ravaged by scavengers. She was in pieces.

But look at her now; she's lovely again. Lovely, lovely, lovely."

"She doesn't belong here! The guards…"

"The King is the one that brought her. He ordered me to fix her for his wife, the Queen."

"The Queen has been missing for over a hundred years, Papa."

"That's right. That's right. She is. No matter – he paid me well in gold."

"We don't use gold anymore, Papa, and no one's seen the King for a very long time either." The rumor was that he still lived, but he preferred the silence of his tower to his throne in the Great Hall. Her father wasn't listening though; instead he continued to putter around the body on the table, arranging her hair and inspecting the stitches on her upper arms and neck. "Papa."

He looked up at her, the bright blue eyes confused again. "Who are you? Why are you in my workshop?"

"It's me, Mattie."

"I do not know a Mattie."

"Papa, please."

"Why do you call me that? I have no children." He strode forward, pushing her out of the room with his club like hands. "Did that thief send you? The one who's always trying to steal my designs?"

"No!"

"You go and tell your master that I am wise to his little schemes. I know he wants to steal her favor away, but she appreciates quality. Fine things like silk and china, not twigs and straw!" The toymaker kept pushing her back until she bumped into one of the piles of forgotten toys and fell to ground. Broken toys fell around her in a waterfall of debris.

"Papa!"

"GO!"

Mattie fled.

Chapter Two

"What do I do? What do I do?" Mattie murmured. She wandered the castle in shock, trailing her hands along the rough stone walls. "He killed someone. Why would he do that? How *could* he?" Yes, her father had a temper. She suffered his verbal abuse multiple times over the years, and heard him yell at others over simple accidents like bumping into him when they passed by, but she never thought that he would actually hurt someone.

No, Mattie corrected herself. He didn't hurt her. Her father hadn't done anything to the girl except for putting her back together. Someone else must have brought her to him.

Her steps brought her near the entrance to the dungeon and she stopped to stare at the heavy door with its large padlock for a moment. It didn't matter who the girl was or who killed her or why - if the King or his men learned about the body, then they would toss her father through that door. He would either be tortured, or locked up in a cell, or...

They may not be able to die, but there were rumors of a man, a wandering minstrel who had been visiting the castle at the time the Curse took effect. He did something to anger the King, though no one really knew what he did. Talesin and Rordan told her it was just a story when she asked. In retaliation, the King had ordered him torn limb from limb and the pieces scattered about the Castle. Those pieces, once separated from the body, wasted away to nothing, but it was said that his head still lived on, and the King kept it on a shelf in his tower. Regardless of how cruel her Father was to others, he didn't deserve to end up like that for the rest of eternity. She quickly turned down a side corridor that led away from the dungeons.

An idea occurred to her: Rordan and Talesin. They claimed to have been the first ones to figure out how to get over the walls and boasted that they knew every secret the castle held. They might know where the girl came from, and, even if they didn't, she could enlist their help in disposing of the body for they would know the best place to hide it.

She ran down the hall, ignoring the bent over shadows that yelled at her as she passed. There was a tower that they liked to hang out in sometimes and throw stones down at the servants and serfs moving around the bailey. She pushed past the broken door that led to the base of it and ran up the spiral staircase, taking the steps two at a time. She jumped over the last step, calling her friend's names, but only the cries of the bats who roosted there answered her.

Perhaps they were in their rooms near the kitchens then. She sighed and left the tower as quickly as she had arrived, almost sliding down the stairs in her haste. However, their rooms were locked and, when she pounded on the door, no one answered.

Mattie checked their other hiding spots but the brothers weren't there either, and the great hall was empty at this late in the night. She finally climbed over the outer wall, expecting to greet them as they returned from meandering around the forest, but there was no sign of any life on the muddy slope beyond the castle. She stood in the small clearing between the outer walls and the tree line, listening to the roar of the waterfall, and called for them to no avail; the forest continued to remain silent.

Towards the East, on the other side of the mountains, the sky began to turn first grey and then pink with dawn. She cursed to herself. Not even Talesin and Rordan were brave enough to stay out during the daytime – she would have to wait until the following night to find them.

She retreated to the castle proper and found a room not far from her father's workshop to hide from the sun in. She curled up on the floor, pulling her cloak around her tightly to keep her warm, but sleep was elusive and she found her thoughts wandering back to the body again and again. Who was she? How had she been lucky enough to escape the curse that plagued them all? Where there more of her kind hidden away in the depths of the castle somewhere?

Mattie sighed. It didn't matter who she was or where she came from, she reminded herself again. All that mattered was getting rid of her.

To distract herself she began to repeat everything she knew about herself like she did every night. She liked to believe that the ritual kept her memory sharp and prevented her from going mad like her father. But there were so many things she didn't remember from those first chaotic days after the curse had taken effect, and after the fright of seeing the ghost lights in the waterfall she couldn't help but wonder if it helped at all. Still she found herself closing her eyes and reciting all that she remembered.

"My name is Mattie. I am a hundred years, two months and nine days old," She yawned then corrected herself, "No, ten days old." Or was it thirteen? She was far from the room she normally slept in and the scratches she had made in the wall to help her keep count.

"I am the only child of the Toymaker and his wife. His wife died long before the bad times while I was still a babe. My father was a favorite of the Queen. She is the one who convinced the King to take pity on us when the plague came." She couldn't remember the Queen but the rumor was that she'd been quite beautiful. They said that the King was handsome as well, and that they were well matched. Mattie knew better though: Rordan and Talesin told her that the King and the Queen had never been happy together and spent most of their time fighting. "My father created a doll out of a girl's body. He claims it was brought to him, but we can't die, and there's no way out of the castle."

Except for those lights in the waterfall. But she could have been imagining those. Just like she had been imagining things when she had been talking to her mask earlier.

She wasn't sure she could trust herself anymore.

She wasn't sure she could trust anything or anyone.

Chapter Three

"Good morning!" The familiar voice was far too chipper, as someone shook Mattie's shoulder roughly, waking her up. She groaned and opened her eyes to find the brothers, Rordan and Talesin, crouching over her. Goofy grins brightened their otherwise grim faces, and their eyes shined bright with mischief.

They told her once that they were identical twins, but now the only thing about them that was similar was their sandy brown hair. At some point during the chaos after the curse someone had taken a knife to Talesin's face and cut his mouth open to his ears. He had stitched it closed, but the flesh never healed, continuing to seep blood and decay instead. One could even see glimpses of his teeth through the holes when he grinned a certain way. Rordan's cheeks were whole, but he was missing the end of his nose, parts of his ears, and most of his hair.

"You missed the fun last night." Talesin said.

"What fun?" She tried to keep her voice light, even though her heart was pounding. Had someone found the body while she was sleeping?

"The guards spotted someone on the other side of the old bridge. A villager, they think."

"A villager?" She blinked up at them, confused and relieved at the same time. The town on the other side of the ravine was abandoned. Had been since the bad times.

"Yes, a villager. A walking, talking, villager."

"Some survived?"

"It's a big, big world. Of course, some would survive."

First lights in the waterfalls, then a body in the castle, and now a villager at the bridge; what was their world coming to?

Rordan leaned forward and stared at her mask. His gaze tracing the cracks in the fine porcelain. He interrupted his brother's tale with, "What happened to you, love?"

"I slipped on a rock by the falls," She stammered, suddenly embarrassed. "And it broke - but I fixed it!"

"Good girl." He murmured, but his voice was so soft she couldn't quite hear what he said.

"What?"

"Nothing." Rordan looked away, suddenly interested in the beams crisscrossing the ceiling above them like the marks that marred his face.

Talesin frowned at his brother and then Mattie. "I would have thought you would be more excited about this. A villager hasn't been seen in decades!"

She had bigger things to worry about, but it was obvious that Talesin would not be happy until he had a chance to talk about the stupid villager first. "I'm sorry, I'm just waking up." She said, faking a yawn and her interest. "What did he look like? What did he do?"

"Dunno. The guards wouldn't let us get close enough to see him, but from what everyone said, he just paced back on the bridge for a bit, shouted something a couple of times, and then left." Talesin said and Mattie rolled her eyes - all that fuss over nothing. "He probably came up on a dare. They used to do that all the time. Rordan says if he comes back and starts yelling again, he'll yell back at him."

"You can't do that! What if he tried to come over here? Or told the others?" The Villagers had been the ones to trap them here to prevent the curse from spreading.

"He'll probably think it's an echo or something."

"Or he'll think it's a banshee and run for his life. They're not very bright and easy to frighten." Rordan finished.

"How would either of you know? We've been locked up over here for a long time. Maybe they've changed." Mattie asked.

Talesin shrugged. "Pet, we're older than you. We still remember what things were like before the curse. The feasts and festivals for Mabon."

"The bonfires for Samhain." His brother added.

"The ghost stories and tall tales told by the fireplace around Yule. The charms hung over the doors and by the windows. But enough about all of that. We heard you was looking for us last night."

"I was." Mattie drawled out the word, trying to think of how to tell them what she saw. "I need your help with a problem."

"A big problem?" Rordan asked.

Mattie nodded, "Yes."

"Like what? Did you drop a bird's nest on the Captain's head again?"

Talesin snorted and laughed. "That was a good one. The look on his face..."

"No." She sighed. That hadn't been fun at all. They had to run and hide from the Captain for weeks on end, know that if he ever caught them, he would have the skin flayed from their bones. Since the fallout from this could be even worse, it was best to just come out with it. She took a breath to steady herself. "There's a body in my father's workshop."

The laughter stopped. "What?"

"When I broke my mask, I came back to the castle to fix it. I went into my father's workshop and saw that he had started to make a doll."

Talesin shared a look with his brother, "So? The Toymaker used to make dolls all the time."

"But he was using a dead body to make it."

"Ha! That's a good one, pet, but you forgot that we can't die."

"This isn't a joke!"

"Shhh." Rordan pressed a finger against his lips and looked out the door and into the hallway. "Do you want someone to hear you and get the wrong idea?"

"But there really is a body!"

"I don't believe you." Talesin said defiantly. "Look, pet, everyone goes a bit nutty after a while and starts seeing things that aren't really there."

"I know!" Mattie snapped. She wished what she had seen had been a figment of her mind, but she knew it wasn't. The girl was as real as the two brothers before her. She had touched it and felt skin and bone. "But I know what I saw."

"Hmf," Was all Talesin said in response.

"If what you saw was real," Rordan began. "If there really is a body in the Toymaker's workshop, the Guards will..."

"Not if we get rid of it before anyone else can find it."

"No."

"No?" She repeated in shock that he would refuse to help.

"It might be better this way," Talesin's tone was suddenly gentle as he tried to explain. "He's getting older and doesn't remember much of anything or anyone anymore. This might be kinder…"

"He's my father!" She cried out. "He's the only family I have left. I can't lose him."

"He's not…" Rordan started to say, but Talesin shook his head and he fell silent.

Talesin sighed. "Look, if we get caught disposing of it, we will be blamed and we'll be locked away – if not worse. I don't know about you, but I happen to enjoy being able to move around freely and not be chained to a wall or torn asunder and scattered about the castle."

"Fine, then. I'll just do it on my own." Trying to move the body without any help would be hard, but the curse hadn't damaged her body too badly. She turned and left the room, following the corridors back to the outside.

The sun was setting, and the rubble in the outer bailey cast long shadows on the ground. She stood in the shadows of the gate, studying the path to the barn and tried not to let its dim glow affect her too much as she studied the distance from here to there. She was trying to figure out the best way to cross without being spotted, when a hand settled on her shoulder, startling her. Another hand quickly pressed her mask against her mouth to silence her shout of surprise.

Talesin nudged his brother, "Told you we still had it."

"Well, we are the masters." Rordan replied.

"I thought you didn't believe me and didn't want to help." Mattie said when Rordan removed his hand.

"I don't, but Talesin reminded me that we made a promise to keep you safe, and that we always keep our promises."

A promise to what? She'd never heard of this before. "Who was this promise to?"

He shrugged, "It doesn't matter. Now are we going to go look at this dead body or not?"

She led him and his brother to her father's workshop. For the second time in as many days she found herself crouching next to the walls, looking through the gaps in the boards for any sign of the toymaker's presence; just like before, there was none. She pulled open the barn door and ushered the others inside. Before she closed it completely, she peered back the way they came, afraid that someone might have seen them or followed them, but the outer bailey was still empty, and no guards stood on the parapets above. She breathed a sigh of relief.

"Is this where it was supposed to be?" Rordan stood in front of the black curtains at the far side of the workshop.

"Yes." Mattie nodded.

He flung them open with a flourish but the room beyond was empty. The buckets of ice, the mirrors on the walls, the candles… all of it was gone except for the table. "See, I told you that you were just seeing things."

"Just your imagination getting away from you." Talesin added.

"But I didn't imagine it!" Mattie cried. She ran forward and pressed her hands against the table top. "It was right here! I swear!" A thought occurred to her, and she leaned down to look under the table, but, no, the body hadn't rolled off during the day. "He moved it. He was just pretending to be confused and he moved it because he didn't want me to take it."

"He couldn't have moved it by himself, and he doesn't have any friends. Who would have helped him?"

"Maybe it was just a doll." Talesin said, and rubbed her back to soothe her. "The Toymaker liked making dolls before."

"That was for the Queen." Rordan reminded him. "And she's long gone."

"Well, maybe it's a gift for when she returns."

His brother glared at him, "You know that won't happen."

"Maybe the King ordered it then." Talesin guessed again.

"Why would the King want a doll?"

"I imagine it gets pretty lonely in that cold tower of his..."

"That's disgusting." Mattie wrinkled her nose and both of her friends laughed.

Rordan took pity on her and changed the subject. "Why don't we go and get some breakfast? Maybe that will make you feel better?"

"I guess." She sighed and let her friends pull her away from the workshop, back to the safety of the inner bailey and the keep that towered over everything. The Great Hall that dominated the bottom floor of the keep was empty except for an old woman with long white hair. She stood next to a fire, stirring the contents of a great pot that hung over it. Rordan grabbed a bowl off a nearby table and emptied the contents out on the floor before holding it out to the crone to fill.

The old woman frowned at both him and Talesin as she doled out their porridge. "Filthy, filthy." The brothers ignored her and she shook her head, still frowning in distaste. When Mattie went to step around her, she looked up, her eyes alarmingly bright despite her apparent age. "Don't you want some, dearie?"

"No, thank you." Mattie eyed the slimy grey porridge and shook her head. She'd found nuts and berries in the forest last night and would feast off that instead.

"Suit yourself."

Mattie lingered for a moment, studying the crone's lined face. She looked familiar, but at the same time Mattie was sure she'd never seen her before. "Do I know you?"

"No, dearie." The crone shook her head. "You've never seen me before now."

"Oh." The sensation began to fade, easing from her mind like the fog burning off in the morning light. She let Talesin grab her hand and pull her away but when Mattie turned around to look back, the crone was gone.

They heard the whispers while they sat in the great hall; the Villager was back and was pacing at the end of the broken bridge again. There was nothing to fear, the guards reassured the panicked faces that turned to them at the news. There was no way for the Villager to cross the ravine and, as long as they stayed out of sight, he would not know that they were here.

Talesin and Rordan smiled at each other and quickly gulped down the remaining porridge. Mattie watched them from behind her mask, "What are you two plotting?"

"Mischief," Rordan said as he stood. "Care to come along?"

"I need to find out what my father did with the…" She caught herself and glanced around, aware that more of the castle inhabitants were waking and filling in the space around them as the moon inched higher across the sky. "The thing… so we can get…"

Talesin pulled her to her feet. "Enough worrying about things that aren't there. Live a little."

A large guard, his forehead cut open from a long ago wound stopped them at the door. "Where are you lot off too?"

"Nowhere sir," Rordan bowed low even though the man bore no rank on his shoulders. "Just off to see if we might be able to catch a bat or two for the pot."

"The bats woke hours ago."

"We plan to wait for them to return."

The man laughed, "And surprise them in the daytime? The sun will burn your hide off your bones if you do that."

"Not in the spot we know…" Talesin crept closer, lowering his voice conspiratorially. "Near the old royal rooms, there's linen closet where they sometimes roost. We were going to wait there for them."

"No one is allowed near the royal rooms!" The guard barked.

"What is going on here?" Two of his friends came to join him, drawn over by his shouts. They stood with their hands on their swords and blocked the door with their combined girth.

"These three were going to visit the Royal rooms and wait for bats." The first guard said.

"No bats there." Replied one. "Haven't been in years."

The other eyed Mattie appreciatively. "Who are you little one? We've not seen your face before." He leaned down, his rank breath making her gag behind her mask. She did not reply, choosing to hide behind Talesin and Rordan instead. He sneered. "Your friend isn't very friendly. Perhaps we should teach her some manners."

The other one pulled out his belt knife, "Perhaps she'll talk once we..."

"No, no. No need for that." Talesin held up his hands pleadingly. "She just... she..."

"She can't speak." Rordan leapt to his rescue. "She lost her jaw during the bad times. That's why she wears the mask you see."

"Old Leroy here." The guard pointed to the man on his right. "Lost his jaw and his tongue, and you don't see him wearing a mask."

"Well, her father is the toymaker, and you know how he is."

"Ah." The guard grunted in reply, he gave his friend a nod and the other man slipped his belt knife away with a disappointed sigh. "Now, where were you off too again?"

"The towers, to catch bats since the Royal chambers are empty of them."

"No. The King's orders are that all must stay inside the hall and keep quiet until the Villager goes away."

"But the Villager is down at the old bridge! That's half a mile from here! He can't hear or see anything we..." Talesin growled in frustration.

The first guard pulled out his belt knight again, pressing it against Talesin's neck. "Do not question the King's orders."

"Yes sir. Sorry sir." Rordan apologized for his brother's actions. He put his hand on Talesin's shoulder and turned him around, leading him and Mattie away from the door and back towards the others.

Talesin cursed, and pressed his hand against the small cut the guard had made. His fingers came away dark with black blood. "What did you do that for? We could have run past them!"

"And spent the rest of our night running? No thank you!" He led them through the maze of tables until they were lost in the crowd and the Guards could no longer spot them. "Besides, there's more than one way out of this joint!" He turned and darted through a door in the wall near the corner of the room. It was hidden by shadows, and broken chairs and tables were piled up on either side of it.

"That's right! The kitchens!" His brother laughed. He grabbed Mattie's hand, "C'mon."

"Not the kitchens!" She cried. The chef was down there. He slaved over long cold fires, still cooking meals out of heavens knew what for a King and a Queen that would never eat them. Where her father might have his bouts where he forgot where and who he was, and who the others were, at least he still understood that the people around him were just that - people. The Chef was so lost to his madness that he did not recognize anything anymore. She did not want to be accidentally mistaken for a chicken and added to a stew.

However, Talesin would not release her despite her pleas. He glanced once over his shoulder to make sure the Guards were not looking, and dragged her behind him through the doorway and down the steep steps. Rordan was waiting for them at the bottom. He pressed a finger to his lips, and then all three of them were darting past the tables stacked with cracked dishes and the skeletal remains of animals that hadn't lived in over a century.

Mattie flinched at every shadow, just waiting for the lumbering Chef to lunge at them. And she swore that every sound was him plotting what he would do with them.

They reached another door – this one was swollen shut by dampness and age. Rordan tugged on the handle uselessly. "Well, damn."

"Maybe if we both run at it, we can knock it lose." Talesin suggested. They both stepped back and charged at the door, crashing into it with their shoulders. The door did not budge, but the loud thud from their impact reverberated around the dark and dusty kitchens.

"Hurry!" Mattie hissed as she kept an eye out for the Chef.

Her friends ran at the door again, and fell to the ground again, groaning in pain. Again, and again, they attacked the door, but it would not budge. At this rate, Mattie thought, they would break their shoulders before it gave way.

Rordan rubbed at his shoulder as he surveyed the offending object that blocked their way. "Maybe if we removed the pin from the hinges?"

"How?" Talesin scratched at the rust around the iron hinges with a finger nail.

"A knife?"

One of the brothers produced a short belt knife from on his person and started chipping away at the rust that fused the hinges shut. Soon there was enough of a gap that he could slip his blade between the pin and the rest of the hinge. He twisted it, and the pin lifted a few inches, groaning and screeching in complaint.

While they worked, Mattie kept watch. A shadow to her left caught her eye. It seemed to be twitching slightly in time with the brother's work on the door - up and down, up and down - almost as if it was breathing... No, that couldn't be possible, shadows didn't breathe. She blinked and wiped a grimy hand over her eyes. When she looked again, the shadow was still moving, but this time the dark mass was rolling, turning, in their direction. "Hurry!"

"Just one more." Rordan said as he stood and went to work on the next hinge.

"There's no time!" She hissed.

"What do you mean?"

"He's here."

"Who's here?"

"The Chef!"

Rordan paused in his work to look around, "I don't see anyone."

The shadow lunged at them with hands outstretched and fingers grasping.

Rordan yelped and they scattered - running in different directions. Unable to turn and or stop his forward motion, the Chef collided with the door they'd been struggling to open. The ancient wood creaked underneath this new attack.

Mattie dove under a table. She peered out from her hiding spot at the Chef as he pushed himself away from the door and turned around. The door started to crack under the abuse, the torch light from outside revealing the Chef's diseased and burnt face. Black fluid oozed from the boils covering his cheeks and heavy sides, dripping on the floor with sickening wet splats as he moved.

She wrinkled her nose at the smell and held his breath as he passed by her table. How would they escape? They could not return to the Great Hall for fear of alarming the guards, but they could not stay here and be turned into tomorrow's 'dinner'.

A hand grabbed her shoulder. She twisted to avoid its grasp only to find that it was Talesin. He pressed a finger against his lips, reminding her to stay quiet. "Where's Rordan...?"

"Over there." He pointed at the cabinets along the wall next to the door. His brother had somehow twisted himself into the narrow empty space. "We need to get out of here..."

"The door is cracking." She whispered as an idea occurred to her. "Maybe if we ran at it now..."

He shook his head. "Not enough time. The Chef would be on us..."

"He's not that fast! We were able to hide before he could turn around!"

"Then why are we still hiding if we can get away so easily?"

"I... well..." She sputtered. Why were they hiding if he was so easy to escape after all? "We didn't know, and he's bigger than we are, and..."

Talesin patted her on the arm. "Don't worry your pretty little head over it." He gestured in Rordan's direction, motioning for his brother to follow their lead. "C'mon. Here we go!"

They bolted out of their hiding spots, and ran towards the door, knocking over pots and pans in their rush to reach it before the Chef grabbed them. Mattie shoved her shoulder into the door along with her friends, and it gave way a little more beneath their combined weight.

The ground shuddered under their feet as the Chef began to lumber towards them again. Mattie paled underneath her mask; even if he was slow, he was bigger and stronger than them. If he caught them... She shook her head to clear her thoughts. "One more time!"

They ran at the door again, and this time it broke apart under their attack. They fell through the opening and into the castles overgrown herb garden. The Chef, too large to pass through the doorway, shoved a meaty arm through and tried to grab their legs. They quickly scrambled away, collapsing against the far wall as the Chef whined and moaned and lamented the loss of his 'dinner'.

"See? That wasn't so bad!" Talesin said.

"If that wasn't so bad, I'd hate to see your idea of worse." Rordan coughed, spitting out pieces of wood and dirt from their fall. "C'mon, we should leave before the guards decide to come and see what caused that noise."

Mattie sighed and followed them through the maze of other yards until they were once again inside the Castle. They climbed over the crumbling outer wall and down into the forest. She turned to the right, to follow the wall to the outer gate and the road, but Rordan shook his head, "Straight down is faster."

"But the road is safer."

"The guards will be using it, and I don't feel like being asked awkward questions, do you?" He waggled his eyebrows.

Mattie eyed the forest before them with trepidation. The moon had not yet risen, and the tall pines were bathed in darkness. She knew that near the castle the ground was mostly level, but further away the slope became steeper, until one needed to be careful where they stepped or risk slipping and tumbling over the edge.

Her friends had already taken off though, running between the trees without a care in the world. She sighed and followed them at a slower pace. It had rained at some point during the day, and the ground underfoot was muddy, making the going even more treacherous than usual. She used the trees to steady her descent as she half walked, half slid until down the slope until she reached the old bridge that once linked the castle to the rest of the world.

The wooden beams stuck out over the ravine, the ends charred from where the Villagers had set fire to it after blocking up the Castle gates. A lantern bobbed back and forth on the other side, but the person holding it was little more than a shadow against the even darker forest. A thin layer of damp muck clung to her leggings, hands, and shirtsleeves, and Mattie shivered in the wind. She ignored her discomfort and squinted, trying to see details. She stepped out onto the bridge to get a better look, and it groaned under her weight. The man's head snapped towards her, but Talesin reached up and pulled her down to the ground next to him. They hid behind the short stone wall that stretched out on either side of the bridge for a small distance. "Careful. He almost saw you."

Mattie nodded, that had been close. She peeked over the wall and, even though she couldn't see his face, she could swear that he was looking in their direction. She slid back down with a shiver. Talesin raised his eyebrows at her. "Are you scared or something?"

"No."

He began to cluck like a chicken in her ear. Mattie flinched away and he giggled. "Prove it. Say something to him."

"Like what?"

"I dunno. He's looking for someone so moan or something."

"Letty? Can you hear me?" He called, his voice echoing through the ravine below them. He stood, waiting for a response for a few minutes. Finally, he was about to turn away when Mattie cupped her hands around her mouth and whimpered. "Is someone there?"

She moaned again in response.

"Letty! Hold on!"

Rordan stopped Mattie before she could moan a third time. "You'd better stop now, before he gets too excited."

"This was your idea." Talesin whined.

"Yeah, but I wasn't actually going to do anything."

"Why not? This is the most fun we've had in ages! And it's not like he can get over here..."

While the brothers argued, Mattie peaked over the top of the wall again. On the other side of the ravine, the villager dropped to his knees and began to rummage through a bag he had strapped to his back. He pulled out something that glinted in the light of his lantern, but before she could see what it was, he stood up and started to swing it around his head. "What is he doing?"

"What?" Talesin asked and glanced over the wall himself. "Get down!"

The villager released the object. It went flew over their heads and landed with a soft thunk in the dirt just a few feet away from where they hid. Mattie inched forward and studied it. It was a rudimentary grappling hook: a rust covered metal rod had three hooks sticking out perpendicular to the top, and a rope was tied to the bottom.

"What was that you were saying? 'It's not like he can get over here'?" Rordan mimicked Talesin's voice.

"Just because he's a good shot doesn't mean he has the bullocks to swing over here."

"It looks like he's going to try." The rope that was tied to the grappling hook began to twitch, and the hook was pulled backwards. It bounced over the ground until it became stuck against the wall with a loud screech that reminded Mattie of... something from a long time ago. The grappling hook continued to grind into the wall as her friends argued. Mattie clasped her hands over her ears to block the noise out as she struggled to remember, the memories surfacing in fragments.

... An axe blade being sharpened on a whetstone...

Talesin cursed. "We need to warn the others!"

... Fingernails clawing at the stone around a metal pole...

"Why? If we do they'll blame us. Do you really want to be locked up with him?"

... A man looming over her, his face in shadow...

"Well at the very least we should hide."

... The glint of a blade...

"I have a better idea." Rordan held up his knife, and Mattie unconsciously flinched away from him. Neither he nor his brother noticed as he sawed at the rope with the knife. Finally, it separated from the grappling hook, and slithered over the edge while the hook fell to the ground with a clang.

"That was close, wasn't it?" Talesin clasped her shoulder, "Are you alright, pet? You look as if you've seen a ghost."

"I'm fine, but what about him?" Mattie lied. She shook her head to clear the flashes from her mind, and jerked her head towards the ravine.

"What about him?"

"What if he fell?"

"Then good riddance." Rordan snorted.

"But what if others come looking for him?"

"Then they'll find his broken body at the bottom of the ravine and assume he had an unfortunate accident." Talesin slid his arm around her and gave her a hug. "Don't worry, pet, we'll keep you safe from the big bad villagers!"

"I'm not afraid of a silly old villager!"

"You're shaking in your boots!"

So, he had noticed her trembling. She shoved him away, "I wasn't the one panicking about what to do unlike someone…"

"Someone who happens to be sitting right next to you?" Rordan asked, his blue eyes flashing with mirth.

"Hey now!" Talesin yelped defensively.

"At least your brother was able to keep his wits about him. Maybe he'll be the one to protect you!"

Rordan tipped his head back and laughed, and Talesin punched him in the arm. Rordan shoved Talesin's head down into the dirt in retaliation, and soon the two brothers were wrestling. Curses and fists were flung around aimlessly, looking for a bit of soft skin to target. They would be black and blue tomorrow.

Mattie scooted backwards to avoid their swinging limbs. Was the villager really gone? She hadn't heard him scream or curse as he fell. Even the ones who threw themselves from the castle towers when the curse had first taken hold had cried out as the ground rushed towards them. She peaked back over the wall.

He was still there.

"He's alive." She murmured.

"You're seeing things again." Rordan jumped up from where he had pinned his brother and joined her. His eyes shot upwards when he saw that she spoke the truth. "Lucky bastard."

"No, smart bastard." Talesin corrected his brother. "You should've known that he wouldn't come over here without tying off the rope on his side, or testing it first."

They watched as the villager squatted at the end of the old bridge, inspecting the end of his rope in the dim light cast by the lantern. He turned it this way and that in his hands and rubbed the end between his fingers.

"He knows." Mattie said.

"Nonsense." One of her friends replied. "He probably thinks it was ripped apart by a rock…"

"Or the rope wasn't strong enough to begin with and snapped." The other one added.

"Even if he does suspect that the rope was cut, your howling would have put the fear of the unknown into his bones. He won't try again."

"I doubt that," She murmured to herself. Her fake moans of pain had been what had led him to try to cross in the first place – if she'd just kept quiet instead of letting her friends goad her into responding to his shouts…

The villager stood and pushed his hair out of his face… hair that gleamed copper in the light of the rising moon.

Chapter Four

The trek back to Mill-On-Rye from Castle Bridge was an hour by foot on a good day. However tonight, with the old road being covered in a river of mire, it took Liam Mercat nearly two hours before he saw the lights of the village on the horizon.

Next time, he would bring his horse with him. A horse would make the trip quicker, and allow him to bring more supplies. He had forgone a mount when he first started searching for her for fear of missing any sign that his sister might have left behind. After tonight, though, he was sure that the answer to her disappearance lay in the old castle so there was no need to toil over every bent leaf and broken branch.

A part of Liam had known all along that he would find her there; Letty was fascinated by the castle that was built into the mountain. Stories ran rampant through Mill-On-Rye that it was haunted by a vengeful king who had murdered all his subjects after he discovered that his Queen had an affair with a traveling minstrel. As a girl, Letty loved sit next to their father in front of the fireplace, begging him for one more story about the King and his adulterous Queen before bedtime. She hadn't lost her fondness for the place as she grew older, and Liam had lost count of the times that they carried a basket out to the old bridge and picnicked with their legs dangling over the edge. They used to spend hours wondering what treasures the old castle held as they ate their meal.

Then, two weeks ago, their father announced that it was time for Letty to grow up and marry a man he had picked for her. To say that Letty was less than pleased was a gross understatement. She threw a tantrum that would make their two-year-old niece embarrassed, then disappeared into the night later that evening.

Everyone, including Liam, believed that she had run away rather than marry a man she didn't care for. While their father looked for her at their Aunt's house in Kybert, Liam had followed his gut and trekked up to the old bridge to search for her there. The bridge had been destroyed ages ago, so there was no way for her to cross, but there were plenty of places for her to hide along the edge. However, he'd yet to find any sign of her presence aside from a piece of her cape clinging to the bottom branch of a bush near the waterfalls.

He had been about to give up hope of ever finding her when, yesterday, he stayed out later than he planned to and saw a girl wandering through the mist on the other side of the ravine. For a moment, he thought that the castle really was haunted like his father insisted, but the girl appeared to be solid as he was.

However, no one would listen to him when he returned to Mill-On-Rye and so he had gone back to the old bridge by himself with only the rope he borrowed from his father's shop, his grandfather's knife, and a grappling hook he found in the ruins near the bridge many years before.

Tonight held even more surprises for him: someone had responded to his shouts, and when he tried to cross, his rope was cut. He ran his thumb across the clean end again; he would like to see someone try to explain that away.

He paused at the edge of the barren fields that surrounded the village for a moment, surveying the place that had been his home for all of his twenty-two years of life. Several decades ago, long before he had been born, a plague passed through the area and nearly wiped out the population. Several mass graves dotted the woods surrounding the town as a testament to those dark days, but Mill-On-Rye had survived where others had fallen. It was a small town, filled with narrow houses that were built so close to each other that a person could lean out their window and touch the wall of their neighbor's house. How the plague didn't pass through like gossip did from one ear to another was beyond him, yet somehow it had.

Despite the late hour a few lights still flickered here and there in the windows, but thankfully his family's house, the largest in Mill-On-Rye, was dark. He would not have to suffer through an interrogation by his mother tonight.

Suddenly exhausted, Liam strode through the streets quickly, not caring who might see him. The busybodies would be gossiping about him and his family tomorrow regardless of what he did. They were the town's favorite topic of conversation after what Letty had done, and, since nothing exciting ever happened in Mill-On-Rye, he imagined that they would continue to be so for a long, long time.

"Young Liam, what are you doing out and about?" A gravely old voice called to him as he passed.

Liam paused and turned to find old Marley watching him from the porch of his house. Ancient, with tan wrinkled skin and white wispy hair that was almost translucent, the man worked a pile of straw by his feet into fantastic shapes and designs with his gnarled fingers. "Everyone is usually in their bed by now."

Liam could ask the man the same question, but Marley was nearly a hundred years old and Liam's mother would have his hide if she learned that he had been rude to a town elder. "Good evening, sir."

"Have you been looking for your sister again?"

"Yes sir."

"By the old bridge?"

"How did you..."

Marley pointed a crooked finger down the road. "Nothing that way except for the bridge and the castle on the other side, so where else would you be coming from?" He returned to knotting the straw. "You don't think she's hiding up there do you?"

"I don't know, sir. She might be."

"Bad place, that."

"Letty's a smart girl. She knows how to survive..." Liam leapt to his sister's defense but Marley shook his head.

"Your grandfather was a great hunter. I know he taught you both well, just like his father taught him, but there are things there and in these woods that aren't human. Things your skills can't protect you from."

"I know about the Ghosts, sir." After the King had killed his wife and his subjects, supposedly their spirits lingered on and still roamed the castle walls to this day. Letty had always shivered with delight when their grandfather reached that part of the story. "But that's just an old wives' tale - they aren't real."

"I wasn't talking about the ghosts, boy. There are darker things about. You've heard the stories about the things that go missing. How grain and other crops that disappear in the middle of the night?"

"It's just rats and other pests..."

"Do you think rats made off with that barrel of dried fish that went missing from your father's store last spring?"

"No, sir, but there was that group of gypsies camping nearby."

"Feh! Blame it on the gypsies... they always do... But it's not. It's them. They ones they said they locked up over there..."

"Who? The gypsies?"

"No, the undying ones, ya daft fool! My father said his father and the others trapped them there, but I've seen things creeping about at night."

Liam sighed.

"Still don't believe me, eh? Do you remember, about five winters ago, when two of our men went hunting up that way and never returned?" Marley reached down to pull up another strand of straw and add it to his creation.

"Yes." In the spring, another group of hunters had found their mangled and half eaten bodies. Liam's mother refused to let him or his sister leave the town until the bear that supposedly attacked the men had been tracked down and killed. It's hide now hung on the wall in the Two Stags pub next to a plaque memorializing the hunters. "They caught the animal..."

"If you believe that tale, you're dimmer than I thought. A bear didn't attack those men, something else did. I saw the teeth marks - they were human. If your sister did go out that way, then I guarantee that thing and its friends have gotten her." He made one final knot in the straw and turned the intricate design around in his hands, ignoring how his young friend's expression grew darker with every word he said.

"Letty is not dead." Liam growled. "There was a girl out there, and if she could survive, then Letty can too."

"What?" Marley looked up, his normally rheumy eyes suddenly clear and bright. "What did you say, boy?"

"There was a girl at the ravine. She had dark hair and a white face..."

"On our side, or on the castle side?"

"Castle side."

"Did she see you?"

"No."

"Good. Good."   The old man heaved a sigh of relief and stood up. "I wouldn't suggest going out there again, young Liam. The next time you do, you might not be so lucky."

"What if she's seen..."

"I know it's hard, but you'd better accept she's gone and move on with your life." He held out his creation for Liam to take. "Here."

The straw charm consisted of a cross woven inside of a circle, with strange designs around its edge. "What's this for?"

"In case something followed you back."

Chapter Five

"Copper hair. The villager had copper hair. Just like the body on my father's table." Mattie murmured as she paced the perimeter of her room. She and her friends had retreated here after the encounter at the old bridge, barely escaping the guards that patrolled the hillside and the castle walls.

"It could be just a coincidence – lots of people have red hair after all. There's…" Talesin stopped as quickly as he began, unable to think of a single person with red hair in the castle.

Rordan rolled his eyes. "Never mind that. Who cares what his hair was. There isn't a body. You were just imagining it. Remember?"

For a moment, she was tempted to give in and admit that he was right. There had been those lights she'd seen in the waterfall, and then there were those flashes of… dreams - no, they felt too real for that - that she experienced while at the bridge. Perhaps she was beginning to go mad like her father after all.

However, something in her friend's tone irked her. It was almost condescending, like she was a little child and he was trying to convince her that there wasn't a monster under the bed. "For the last time, I know what I saw."

"Maybe she isn't imagining it like you say. Maybe she's become a seer." Rordan suggested, speaking as if Mattie wasn't standing there in front of him.

"That's not possible." His brother argued. "There's no such thing as seers."

"They said there was no such thing as witches either and look at us now - cursed by a witch!"

"Neither of you are helping!" Mattie cried out in frustration.

"Well, what do you expect us to do?" Talesin asked. "Look for a body that doesn't exist?"

"I said I know what I saw."

"Fine. Say there is a body after all... What does it matter where it is? It's no longer in your father's workshop, so if the guards somehow find it they can't blame him. He's safe. That's what you wanted right?"

"Yes, but how did it get here?"

"Who cares?"

"I do. If that villager almost made it over tonight, then who's to say that she didn't?"

"Girls don't use hooks like that Villager was using. And there's no other way across."

"Maybe she climbed down the ravine and back up the other side..." But, no, that didn't seem plausible either; the girl's hands had been soft and smooth, as if she'd never done a day of hard work in her life. If she had climbed down the ravine, there would have been blisters and calluses marring her palms. Mattie began to pace again as she tried to think of other ways the girl could have made it across to the castle.

"Maybe a giant bird carried her across." Rordan suggested.

She scoffed. "Don't be absurd."

"It's late, what do expect?" Talesin yawned as he stood. He crossed the room, opened the door, and peered out into the hallway. After a moment then motioned for his brother to follow him.

"Where are you two going?" Mattie asked.

"To bed."

They were abandoning her? In her hour of need? "But we have to figure out where the body..."

"No, we don't." He sighed.

"But what if there's a way across that we don't know about? What if others find it out?"

"Let it go, Mattie." He kissed the top of her head. "We'll see you in the great hall tomorrow. Sleep tight." Then he and his brother were gone, leaving her alone with her thoughts.

She plopped down in her chair with a sigh. Talesin was right; she should be happy that the body was no longer in her father's workshop, and that he was safe. However, the mystery of it continued to bother her - villagers didn't just show up at the castle out of nowhere and dead bodies couldn't just get up and walk away on their own. She snorted and corrected her thoughts: no, thanks to the curse bodies could get up and move about even after death, but this one had been really dead.

Hadn't it?

Was it possible that the body had become one of them upon death? That she was out there wandering around the castle by herself? Everyone in the Castle had been cursed at the same time, but perhaps the spell still lingered in the air and affected anything that might encounter it.

It still didn't explain where the body came from though.

Mattie yawned. Talesin was right - the hour was late, and it was beginning to affect her cognitive skills; dead bodies walking, curses lingering, villagers haunting the bridge. What was she thinking. She chortled to herself sleepily and pushed herself up from her chair. She took the bit of charred wood that she kept nearby, searched the walls until she found an empty spot, and made a mark with the wood. She stepped back and surveyed her work. "My name is Mattie. I am a hundred years, two months and twelve days old..."

Mattie woke late the next day. The sun had already set, and the moon was already high in the sky as she left her room and headed for the Great Hall. However, when she reached it, the cavernous space was empty. The massive cauldron where the gruel was made and doled out was empty, and the fire that normally burned underneath it was out. She called out thinking that someone might be hiding in the shadows, but no one responded to her cries.

Had something happened? But no, there were no signs of struggles or battles like there had been during the dark times.

And then she saw the black stain.

It started near the door to the kitchens and here and there smaller streaks marked the floor until it finally stopped at the foot of the King's dais. Here the stain spread into a large puddle and smaller strands branched off to follow the mortar between the stones in the ground. Mattie knelt and ran a finger through it; blood.

Whatever had happened had happened recently, for it was still fresh and warm, it's metallic odor filling the air.

Mattie hurried out of the Great Hall and wandered the hallways, looking for the others, but the corridors were just as still as the empty space she'd just left. There were no guards patrolling the Castle, and even the mindless ones were silent. Where was everyone?

Finally, as she passed a window, she heard voices. She pushed her way through the empty frame and landed in a pile of leaves and other debris. There, just ahead, stood the rest of the castle denizens. They gathered in groups, their faces paler than normal and filled with shock and fear while guards watched from the parapets that surrounded them.

Mattie drifted close to one of the groups in hopes of overhearing what had happened. She caught snatches of conversations as they spoke in hushed voices.

"...tied him up earlier today..."

"...torn apart..."

"... his head just hangs there, chomping at nothing - can't even speak the poor thing..."

".... well he never spoke much to begin with anyways... Always babbling about this or that..."

Mattie felt her heart begin to pound against her chest. Had her fears been realized? Had the guards discovered the body and punished her father for it? Or had they learned that she and the others had antagonized the villager and torn her friends apart? "Who was tied up?" She asked them. "Who did the guards get?"

The group of men and women just stared at her, their eyes suspicious and their expressions unwelcome. Stunned by the animosity, Mattie backed up against the wall and pulled her hood over her head as if it would protect her from their anger.

"It was her fault... I saw her go down there with those friends of hers..." One of them whispered to another as she turned away.

"Troublemaker, just like her father."

"Haven't seen him in a while though..."

"Good riddance."

Mattie approached another group and to glean more information from their conversation, but they all fell silent when she drew near. "Has anyone seen Talesin? Or Rordan?"

Just like the others they did not answer. They glared at her and then turned their backs.

She left them and walked quickly towards the front of the keep. In the past, the King had stuck the heads of his enemies on pikes overlooking the castle gates for all to see. If the guards kept up that tradition, then the head of whoever they'd punished would be hanging there as well. Since the others would not answer her, the only way to find out who the victim was for her to take a look herself.

Just like her experience at the bridge, she was suddenly struck by a vision that consumed her senses. This one, however, was clearer and longer instead of bits and pieces.

She looked down at the heads of the King's enemies from a great height. They had begun to rot: their tongues protruding from cracked lips, missing eyeballs and other pieces of flesh that had been pecked away by crows long ago. The stench threatened to overwhelm her and she tried to turn away. However, no matter how hard she tried to escape, she could not; the person who had dragged her there against her wishes, had trapped her against the parapets and held her head firm so she was unable to look away from the disgusting sight.

"See what happens those who cross him? Mend your ways or end up like them!"

"He would never do that to me!"

"Really? You're replaceable to him - just like the others." Her captor finally let her go. He stepped around her to lean against the parapets himself and look down at the heads. "Just like me." All she could see was his profile. Outlined by the setting sun, it was strong and handsome, the face of a leader.... and then he turned to look at her, revealing that the other half of his face was heavily scarred. Claw marks ran from his forehead down to his chin. They bisected his eyebrow, cheek, and lip in deep angry red lines. "Don't continue with this madness... tell him to leave, for his and for your safety. Please, Iso..."

A hand darted out of the shadows, pulling her into a little alcove and startling her out of her vision. "You don't want to see that, pet." She yelped and the familiar voice shushed her. "It's only me."

"Talesin!" Mattie hugged him tightly.

He chuckled, "The one and only."

"I thought... From the way everyone was speaking..."

"No, no. They didn't get us. We're fine."

"Father?"

"He's around here somewhere."

"Then who did they get?"

"The chef.

"What? Why?"

"He was a liability. They said he made noise when the Guards asked for silence, and then he escaped when they told us to stay indoors."

"But he wouldn't have if we hadn't gone down there. He was only chasing after us!"

"I know. I know."

"We should say something…"

"And end up like him? I happen to like my head where it's at, thank you very much."

"Then we should stand up to them. We can't keep living in fear and letting them walk all over us like this!"

He shushed her, glancing around to make sure no one else had heard her outburst. "I don't know if you've noticed, but there are more of them than there are of us."

"But…"

"They're also still well fed and have their wits about them."

"… We can't…"

"No! no more!" Talesin shouted.

Mattie flinched - he had never yelled at her before. Never. She stepped away from him, but he grabbed her hand, his expression suddenly apologetic. "Mattie, wait… I didn't mean to snap… We're only trying to keep you…"

"…Safe." She finished for him. "I remember that stupid promise."

He looked surprised. "You do? But we never… You weren't there…"

"You mentioned it last night, remember?" She jerked her hand away from him. "Well, you can forget about it - I'm perfectly capable of taking care of myself."

"Mattie…" He sighed, but before he could say another word, she turned and ran back into the castle keep.

Chapter Six

Talesin was right, Mattie realized after she had stewed over the problem for several hours. As much as she might hate the Guards oppression, there was no way to overthrow them. They did outnumber the rest of the castle citizens four to one, they were better fed, and they were smarter and more aware of their surroundings than everyone else. Perhaps if the King ever came out of his exile - if he was even still alive, that was - he might be able to control them, but until then the rest of them were at the Guard's mercy.

She also knew she shouldn't have spouted off to Talesin like she did. Yes, she was more than capable of taking care of herself, but he and Rordan had done so much for her over the years... Without their help, she would not have been able to survive as long as she had; they had shared food with her when she was hungry, taught her to hunt and trap, and how to move about the castle unseen. If it hadn't been for them, she would have been strung up in the dungeon or lost her head like the Chef long ago.

And how long would she be able to take care of herself if these visions kept up? There had only been two so far, but they had been so real and intense. How much longer did she have before they consumed her completely and she began to wander the halls like the other lost souls?

Mattie forced herself to her feet and began the long walk to the other side of the Castle.

As she drew near she could see the dilapidated and warped door that led to their room hung open on its hinges, and firelight painted shadows on the wall. Good, she thought to herself, she wouldn't have to spend the rest of her night running around searching for them like she had two days ago.

As she drew near she could hear the two brothers yelling at each other, their voices echoing out into the hallway.

"This is all your fault!" Rordan's voice, normally so soft and quiet, was rough with anger. "Our lives have been nothing but one problem after another since we found her."

Mattie smothered a gasp; had they been the ones to find the body and bring it to her father? Had they also been the ones to move it? She crept closer to their door in an attempt to hear them better.

"It doesn't matter now - what's done is done." Talesin replied

"It matters a lot! I don't want to end up like the chef, with my head on a pike for everyone to see. Do you?" The silence stretched on until Rordan asked again, "Do you?"

"No." His brother finally sighed. "But we promised..."

Mattie frowned as she realized that they were talking about her and not the body like she'd originally thought. Maybe she would finally learn who had asked them to protect her. The man from her vision maybe?

"That stupid promise..." Rordan groaned, echoing her thoughts from earlier.

"We gave our word..."

"I know, I know." Now he was the one sighing. "We should have never agreed to this nonsense. We were fools."

"How we were to know that he'd go mad? Or that we'd be cursed?"

"Even so, we were in over our heads then, and we definitely have no idea what we're doing now."

"We can't give up on her!" Talesin's shout startled Mattie, making her jump. She held her breath and prayed that they did not hear her soft cry of surprise.

"I'm not saying we should! You have to stop trying to impress her though. The guards will notice."

"You went along with it."

"Only because there's no stopping you when you get one of your ideas."

"You're just as bad sometimes."

"Fine. Enough arguing, the sun will be up soon. We need to get moving if we want to do this."

Talesin grumbled something about how it could wait, but Rordan reminded them that their work was important. Mattie blinked in surprise; what work could they be talking about? It wasn't as if there was anything left for them to do...

There were sounds of a scuffle, and then footsteps drew near the doorway. She scrambled backwards, darting to hide in the shadows as her friends entered the hallway. They were dressed in clothing that she had never seen before; it was black like the night and they carried lanterns and bags in their hands. Mattie eased farther back along the wall, expecting them to come her way and see her. However, instead of heading towards the Great Hall or the other communal areas of the Castle, they turned right and headed deeper into the castle itself.

She exhaled in relief, then, rather than returning to her own rooms, she followed them at a distance. She watched as they darted from shadow to shadow and peered around each corner, ever vigilant for the guards in their red tunics. She longed to speak up, to ask them how this was sneaking about was any better than Talesin's attempts to impress her. However, her curiosity about what they were up to made her hold her tongue - there would be a time for questions later.

Suddenly, they turned down another hallway and the air became damper and more familiar. Mattie stared at her surroundings, wondering what they would want with this part of the castle for it had been picked over long ago. They turned again and up ahead loomed a familiar door with many locks - the entrance to the dungeon.

Mattie assumed that it was sealed shut by age like the door in the kitchens, but, to her surprise, Talesin and Rordan stopped in front of it and sat down their supplies. She watched as one lifted the bar blocking it while the other one tugged on the heavy iron ring set into the door. It groaned and complained as it opened, revealing a black empty maw. She waited, expecting the poor souls who had been trapped there when the curse began to come pouring out, but nothing moved in that void.

The two brothers picked up their supplies and glanced about. Mattie hid again, praying that they hadn't seen the white of her mask watching them from the gloom. When she dared to peek around the corner

again, the brothers were gone and the door was closed
and barred once more.

*She was dying. She had known it as soon she saw
the red bumps spreading across her skin. She had prayed,
of course, that she was wrong, that it was just a rash, but
soon she had the fever and the other symptoms followed
quickly.*

*"It's the plague," Her servants whispered to each
other when they thought she couldn't hear. "First the boy
and now her."*

"No one ever survives it." Another said.

"Maybe it's better that way."

*They sent for the doctors anyways, and she'd
been forced to suffer their pokes and prods and made to
drink their noxious potions. It was no use; she continued
to grow sicker and sicker.*

*The physicians were here now, filling her room
with smoke from the incense and other herbs they
insisted on burning. They believed the smoke would keep
the illness away but all it did was make her cough and
each cough sent shooting pains up and down her spine
and ribs. It was torture, but her servants were right: this
was better than what awaited her if she had remained
healthy and whole.*

*She wondered how much longer it would be
before this ended. Every time she closed her eyes, she
prayed that she would not wake up, but then a new
morning dawned revealing that she was still trapped
here.*

*A priest stood over her, the soft click of his rosary
beads and the ancient prayers lulling her back to sleep.*

Please, she prayed before the darkness took her. Please let this be the time.

Mattie woke.

At first, she feared that she might be ill; her clothing, damp from sweat, clung to her skin and she shivered in the chilly air. She, also, felt more than a little disoriented. She stared around her room in confusion, not recognizing the marks she had made on the walls, nor the broken furniture and torn tapestries. Her room was supposed to be cleaner and filled with finer things than this!

And then she remembered; she was only the toymaker daughter, this was her room, she was not ill, but she and the others were forced to live on for eternity thanks to... no one was sure quite what had happened. It didn't matter though - she would survive it just like she survived the plague, and just like she would keep on surviving day in and day out until whenever this madness came to an end. Though, she admitted to herself, if these memories that were not hers kept appearing, she might not escape the bane of time.

But what if the memories were hers?

She laughed at that idea, the sound echoing through the empty room. Yes, there were scars on her ankle - little raised bumps like what she'd seen in the dream - but she had never lived in such an opulent room, or worn nice clothing like that. Her father had been favored by the Queen, and had been well off as a result, but they'd never been rich enough to afford such nice things. He liked to spend his money on supplies instead of on his family...

Or had he? What if there had been nice dresses and jewelry? What if he had done everything to save her by hiring physicians like in the dream?

She struggled to remember, but she realized that in addition to not remembering anything of the bad times, she could not recall any details of her life before the curse. All she knew was only what her friends told her - but after what she had overheard last night, she didn't know if she could trust them anymore.

In anger, she ran her hands over the walls of her room, rubbing the marks she had made over the years into oblivion.

She instantly regretted it. She found her burnt piece of wood and quickly began redoing the marks she'd destroyed.

"My name is Mattie," She started murmuring the reassuring mantra as she worked. "I am a hundred years, two months and twelve days old. I am the Toymaker's Daughter. His wife died when I was but a babe. Rordan and Talesin are my friends. They went to..." The words died on her lips as she recalled what had happened the night before. She had followed the brothers to the bowels of the castle and watched as they opened and walked through the door that led to the dungeons. Afterwards, she had waited outside for them for hours, until, eventually, daylight forced her back to the safety of her room. Perhaps they were back by now...

Forgetting her ritual, she let the charred wood drop from her fingers as she ran from the room.

Chapter Seven

      First, Mattie went to Rordan and Talesin's rooms to see if they were back from wherever they gone the night before. There was no sign of them though; the rooms were cold and still and filled with shadows. She called out their names, believing that perhaps they were just sleeping, but no one answered and nothing moved except for the dust stirred up by her breath.

      Next, she retraced her steps to the dungeon door, hoping to find it ajar, but it was still closed. She tugged on the heavy ring and lock. Despite her best attempts to open it, the door remained stubbornly shut. Finally, she checked the dirt she had spread on the floor in front of it. It was an old hunting trick that Rordan showed her many years ago. He had explained that it could be used to pick up tracks, however the debris she'd scattered about hadn't been disturbed.

      She sighed and stood, wondering what to do next. She could spend her day waiting around for them to return, but who knew how long that would take, and attempting to follow them was obviously not an option.

Her stomach rumbled, reminding her that it had been two days since the last time she ate – if not longer. She sighed to herself, left the dungeon door and its mysteries, and made her way to the great hall.

The large gathering space was busy today though the mood was still somber. People sat around eating and chatting, but whenever someone laughed a little too loudly, they cast frightened looks at the King's men scattered about the room.

"They're afraid." A voice at Mattie's elbow said.

Mattie turned to find the crone from two nights ago standing beside her. Once again, the deep wrinkles lining her face seemed oddly familiar, but she could not place where she'd seen them before. "Can you blame them after what happened?"

"Not at all." The old woman frowned and sighed to herself. "These things often happen when madmen are left to rule. You would think I would be used to it by now. Now enough of that depressing subject - are you hungry?"

"No," Mattie lied. However, her stomach rumbled, revealing her deceit.

The crone cackled and grabbed her hand, dragging her along to the cauldron. "Come! Come! I made a special stew today."

"Oh, okay…"

The stew inside the pot was grey and slimy like the porridge from the other day, but despite the awful smell, Mattie found herself filling up a bowl under the woman's orders.

"Now, I know it won't help the hunger, but it'll…" The crone's voice drifted off as she caught sight of the red pockmarks decorating Mattie's wrist.

"What?" Mattie asked. Everyone carried the bumps on one part of their body or another.

"Nothing... It's just... I... I knew another woman who was touched by the sickness there." She stared up into Mattie's face. "She wore a mask as well. A different type of mask though, one of ice, to protect herself from others."

"What happened to her?" Mattie asked politely, even though she wanted to run far away from the woman. Something about her sudden reverence unnerved her and made her skin crawl.

"No one knows - she disappeared."

"You speak of the Queen." Though, there were others who had gone missing during the dark days, so it was possible that it could be someone else.

"Yes." The old woman confirmed her lucky guess. "Poor thing, poor thing."

For some reason, the mention of the Queen irritated Mattie. Even though it was because of her that she and her father were safe, the Queen had escaped the horror of the curse while they continued to live on through the years. "How is she the poor one? She didn't suffer like the rest of us."

The crone tutted. "This curse of a life is horrible all right, but don't try to compare your woes to someone else's, child - especially when you don't know what they've been through. She may not be here today, but she suffered. Oh, how she suffered. Her whole life was nothing but pain and grief."

"Oh?" Mattie asked, her curiosity piqued. While Talesin and her father were supporters of the Queen, hardly anyone spoke of her anymore.

"She was betrayed, you know. First by her father, then by her husband, and, finally, her people. All because she fell in love with the wrong person." The crone patted her hand absently. "Let's hope it never happens to you."

"I'll never fall in love." Love had no place in this ruined castle or amongst the curse souls living here and anyone who believed otherwise had lost their mind.

The crone laughed at that, long and loud. Her laughter filled the room, echoing among the timbers above them. But to Mattie's surprise, no one glanced their way - not even a guard. "Oh, dearie. Thank you, I needed that. Now go enjoy your dinner." She pushed her towards an empty seat at a table. "Go on... go now."

After eating, Mattie found herself wandering aimlessly about the empty hallways and rooms, straying far from the common areas that she was familiar with. Here was a room that had completely collapsed in on itself. There was one that was marked by flooding. Another was reclaimed by the garden it butted up against; vines wound through the broken glass and up across the ceiling and a carpet of grass and moss covered the floor.

She found a nursery filled with toys that were probably her father's creations. However, they, along with the furniture in the room, had all been destroyed long ago - not by time, but by human hand. Did the King and Queen have a child that was lost to the plague or the curse? Or had they been hoping for one? No one ever spoke of a prince or a princess. Mattie bent to pick up a teddy bear that had been torn apart and sat it on a dusty shelf. The feelings of anger and the sadness that haunted the room was overpowering. It settled in her gut next to the nasty porridge she'd eaten earlier, making it hard to breathe. Mattie left, shutting the door firmly behind her to hide the carnage.

She heard voices in the hallway beyond the nursery, and the soft clink of chain mail.

Guards.

Mattie evaded them by hurrying down the hallway and through an open door. She waited until they passed before she dared to move again.

Once it was safe, she stepped out of the shadows and discovered that she had taken sanctuary inside of a library. Above her windows let in the moonlight, revealing row after row of shelves filled with books. She ran her fingers along the bindings, selected one that looked promising, and sat down on the ground before opening it. The book was tinted with age and stained by mold, but the carefully drawn pictures still shined with golden ink.

She flipped through the pages, her eyes skimming over the familiar letters. To her surprise, she could understand them and the words and sentences they formed. In hindsight, it made sense to her that she would know how to read - perhaps she had helped him keep his books before coins fell out of favor - but she could not remember learning. Surely that was something one wouldn't forget, would they? But there were not many books to be found in the common areas so it wasn't as if she had an excuse to try. She would have to remember that for her nightly litany so she would not forget again.

The book contained a lovely tale about a girl who had been cursed to sleep forever when she pricked her finger on a spindle. Mattie was soon completely enthralled, and lost track of time as she flipped through the brittle pages. She was at the part where the hero and heroine met and realized they were attracted to each other when she heard the footsteps.

Mattie held her breath. Had the guards come back? What if she had wandered someplace she was not meant to be? What if it they found her, and she ended up like the Chef? But she hadn't seen any signs telling her to keep out during her meanderings, and she hadn't run into any locked or boarded up doors. She glanced around the edge of the shelf she'd been sitting against, ready to run.

Instead, the figure passing by the doorway was a girl. A girl with copper colored hair spilling down her back. Clothed in a simple dress and a cloak, she glanced over her shoulder, her sad blue eyes meeting Mattie's grey ones for just a moment. Then she turned and was gone, the dust swirling in the empty void she left behind.

The book Mattie was reading fell to the floor as she stood up and rushed to the door. She glanced in either direction down the corridor looking for the figure, finally spotting the ragged bottom of the other girl's cloak disappearing around a corner.

She ran after it, turning down hallway after hallway, as the girl led her deeper and deeper into the castle. She came close to catching her many times, but the other girl always seemed to be one step ahead no matter how quickly Mattie ran.

The continuous maze of hallways and rooms stopped suddenly, emptying out into a garden lit by the moon and the stars high above. Mattie skidded to a stop in shock as she stared at her surroundings. Despite the disrepair of the rest of the castle, this garden was surprisingly well kept; the plants and flowers were trimmed and contained to their beds instead of reclaiming the paths and far off she could hear the burble of water in a fountain. She followed the trail of stepping stones that stretched out in front of her, her head turning from side to side as she took it all in.

Even though she had never seen it before - any of it - the well-worn walkways between roses and other flowers seemed familiar. Actually, the garden felt more than just familiar. In fact, the longer she stood there, the more she realized that she knew it by heart like the cracks in her mask.

She knew, though she didn't know how to explain how she knew, that if she continued straight ahead there would be a marble fountain topped by a statue of a bird with a tail of long feathers that curved around the sphere he stood on. Beyond that, down a smaller side path, there was a grassy circle which was the perfect place to have a picnic during the summertime, or to watch the stars pass overhead during the night.

Her heart continued to race as if she were still running and the little hairs on the back of her neck stood up as if she had walked into a cold room. It was one thing to not remember that you could read if it had been centuries since you had a reason to do so, but it was another thing entirely to recognize someplace one had never been. Was this more proof that she was losing control of her mind? Like the dreams of the woman dying?

Somewhere nearby branches snapped as someone stepped on them, the sound echoing through the quiet garden. Mattie turned just in time to catch a glimpse of her quarry darting between some topiary a few yards ahead.

She plowed ahead, all worries about her memory forgotten as tried to catch the girl again. But, just like before, the girl proved to be faster. Plants and flowers passed by her in a blur as she ran, and then, suddenly, the fountain she remembered but didn't rose up in front of her. For the second time that evening, she froze in shock.

The water bubbled over the moss stained stone, splashing into a pool at its base. In any other circumstance, the sound would be rather soothing, but Mattie's skin broke out in gooseflesh once again as she tried to ignore the unwanted memories that threatened to overwhelm her.

They made no sense!

She shouldn't have them!

However, they persisted in bubbling to the surface of her mind. She could remember sitting on the edge of this fountain, and trailing her fingers in the water until the shadow of a man fell over her, interrupting her. She could also remember reading aloud while sitting on a bench in a little alcove not far from here to someone who lurked just out of sight...

There was one way to find out if the memories were real or not, she thought to herself. If the fountain was here, then just a few feet away, to her left there would be an alcove that was partially hidden from sight with ferns. She rolled her shoulders back and forced herself to walk towards it, praying all the while that she was wrong. Whatever gods were listening apparently did not hear her, for when she pushed past the ferns, there was the little alcove with its bench.

She bowed her head, cursing herself and her luck while she blinked back tears from her eyes.

Maybe this was all a dream. As soon as the idea occurred to her, she seized on to it. Yes, this had to be a dream. It was a dream. She pinched herself, hissing at the sharp pain. It was real. She closed her eyes, and sighed. Since this was real, then that meant that these were more memories that she had forgotten due to the passing of time. But this place was too nice to have ever been available to her, the only daughter of a lowly merchant. Even if her father was a favorite of the Queen, would she really bring him or his child to a place like this to discuss business?

"May I help you?"

Mattie turned to find a man standing at the end of the path, staring at her with an annoyed expression on his face as if she had interrupted something. Just like the body she had found in her father's workshop, this man was too handsome to be one of them - his nose was straight and solid, and his fair skin was free of any pockmarks. Also, his clothing was finer than anything she had ever seen – soft linens and velvets trimmed in satin.

"I... uhm..." She froze, unsure of what to do.

"I said, may I help you? This is area is private." There was an imperious tone to his voice now that grated on Mattie's nerves.

"I didn't notice a sign telling me to keep out."

"Then a guard should have stopped you."

"Why? What? I didn't see a guard anywhere..." With a jolt, she remembered her task and glanced around, but she could not see the girl anywhere. "Did you see someone come this way?"

"No, you and I are the only ones here."

"She was wearing a cape..."

"I said that you and I are the only ones here!" He walked towards her confidently, his head held high as he believed he owned the castle and everything in it. "Now tell me what you are doing here before I have my men throw you back in the ruins where you belong!"

As he drew closer to her, Mattie saw the scar poking up above the scarf tied around his neck and tucked into his shirt – there was only one Undying One she knew of that had a scar like that.

One man who had had his throat slit and lived.

The King.

Chapter Eight

Mortified at being caught intruding on the King's private sanctum, Mattie dropped to her knees and bowed until her forehead touched the ground, "Your Highness! I'm sorry, I was following someone ..."

He stopped in front of her, the tips of his boots bumping against her fingers. She pulled her hands away from him. "This girl in the cape?"

She grimaced behind her mask. Here she had gone and told him the one thing she hadn't wanted him or the guards to find about. But there was still hope; he didn't know who the red headed girl was or where she came from. "Yes, sir. I'm sorry, sir. I was following her and I didn't realize where I was."

"Mm. I see." The King's voice was growing softer, gentler, like dark smooth velvet. But Mattie knew that that did not mean she was out of danger yet, she could hear the undercurrent of anger still lingering beneath the surface. It wouldn't take much to set it off. She fought the urge to run away from him, willing herself to stay perfectly still for fear of inciting his anger further. "Well, as I explained earlier, there is no one here except for you and me."

"And your men, sir." She could see their feet now out of the corner of her eyes. Dusty, cracked boots hiding in the shadows. How had she missed them earlier? How had they missed her? Oh, she was sure to get it now. If not from the King, then definitely from them - they did not like it when people made fools of them.

"Yes," He admitted. "But no girl in a cape."

Mattie nodded, the chin of her mask scratching against the stepping stones beneath her. "I'm sorry, sir." She apologized again. "I'll leave now."

"No. Not just yet." He reached down and touched her chin and forced her to look up at him. "I know all my people, but you are a stranger to me. Who are you?"

"Mattie, sir. I'm the toymaker's daughter."

"The Toymaker has a daughter?"

"Yes, sir."

"Interesting."

"If you knew your people like you claim you do, you would know that, sir." The words slipped out before she could stop them and she grimaced. That little comment would be the end of her. She knew it. With a flick of his hand he would have her head cut from her neck and add her to the wall next to the chef.

He chuckled instead. It was pleasant sound, and just as rich as his voice. However, despite his apparent mirth, there was something calculating in his expression now. He motioned for her to stand, his eyes skimming over her body, hidden though it was by layers and layers of clothing that was little more than rags.

"I am learning that some of my men are quite good at keeping secrets. Perhaps that is why I never knew of you before today. You are someone's secret. A secret that they want to keep away from me."

"Or..." She licked her lips, unsure of what to say or do next. "I could just be an ordinary girl who made a wrong turn chasing after a ghost."

"Let's see what is under that mask. Perhaps that will hold the answer to our little mystery here." He reached out, his fingers brushing against the bottom of her mask.

Don't let him do it! A new voice hissed in her ear. Mattie jerked away, stumbling backwards. "No!"

"How disappointing." He grunted and stepped away.

"I'm sorry, your highness, but my father refuses to let me remove it."

"Not even for your King?"

"Not even for him."

"How interesting..."

No, no, no, no. The strange voice continued even though the danger was over with for the moment. It was light and airy, barely more than a whisper. Mattie glanced around, but she couldn't find the source. None of the guards nearby were women, and if they were, they were not the type to speak so gently. That left the statues and the King. The statues, obviously, couldn't speak, and the King showed no signs of hearing the voice. *This is all wrong. Leave! Leave now! Get away!*

Mattie bit back a bitter laugh; first she was remembering things she shouldn't, and now she was hearing voices that weren't there. She pressed her fingertips against her eyes.

"Are you alright?" The King asked.

"Yes, sir. I'm fine." She lied. "But I should go now..."

A guard stepped forward before she even finished speaking, "I will take her back to the..."

"No," The King barked, turning his head to glower at the guard. "She stays."

The man bowed, "Yes, my lord."

The King watched him as he silently retreated into the shadows before turning his attention back to Mattie. "Tell me more about yourself, my dear girl who should not be."

"I don't know what to say, sir."

"Oh, I'm sure you have a tale or two to entertain me with. Something not even your best friends know." The King smiled and held out his hand.

Mattie hesitated about taking it. He seemed nice enough now that his rage had eased and he was not teasing her about secrets but the strange voice continued to scream at her to run, to not to trust him. However, as much as she might want to leave, he made it clear that she could not do so until he dismissed her. She eyed the paths around them wondering if she could run like the voice begged her to. However, if she did, he would only send his men after her, and while she was able to sneak past them, she doubted she could outrun them.

A flicker of annoyance crept across his face, "Come now, I don't bite."

"Yes, sir. Sorry, sir." She placed her palm in his and let him pull her deeper into the garden. The King tucked her hand into the crook of his arm. Her heart fluttered strangely again at his touch, so smooth and soft compared to her rough hands.

"Surely there is something interesting that has happened to you recently." He tilted his head to the side, studying her again. Mattie held her breath ready to dart out of the way if he tried to touch it again. "Your mask is cracked. There must be a tale there. What happened to it?"

"I fell by the falls. It slipped off my face, but I fixed it."

"And what was so interesting by the falls?"

"Eggs, sir."

"Eggs? You risked life and limb for eggs?"

She shrugged. "It's been awhile since we've had fresh eggs."

"It's been awhile since we've had fresh anything."

"Yes." Every now and then someone might discover some new cache of food that had been hidden away during the bad times, but those treasures were few and far between.

He sighed, and they passed the next few moments in silence. She did her best to ignore him, which was hard considering how tightly he was holding on to her hand. Instead she glanced around the garden, noting the full branches on the trees overhead, and the flowers blooming along the trail.

"You're not much of a conversationalist, are you?" The King finally spoke, teasing her again.

Mattie shook her head. "No, sir. Aside from Talesin and Rordan I hardly speak to anyone."

"Rordan and Talesin?" There was that chuckle again, crawling through her ears and making her heart beat faster and freeze in fear at the same time. "You know those two troublemakers?"

"They're my friends, sir. My only friends."

"They're my men."

Mattie stopped, struggling to process what he just said. "They're your... men?"

"Aye. Lords, in fact."

Lords? Talesin and Rordan were *nobles*? "But..."

"Do you think I would lie?"

"No! Of course not." She said quickly, lest she anger him again. "It's just, we're very close, sir. Very close. I don't know why they wouldn't tell me something like that."

"Don't be too upset with them; I rather think that they're ashamed of it." He tugged on her arm, pulling her along again, like a stick being battered by a rapid river. "In fact, they fell out of favor many years ago and have yet to redeem themselves."

"Oh," was all Mattie could think of to say.

"I'd be careful with them, my dear. If they could not remain loyal to me, their liege lord, I highly doubt that they would remain loyal to you - a mere slip of a girl." He eyed her again, clearly expecting her to defend them. Mattie wanted to. Really wanted to. Rordan and Talesin would never abandon her. Never. But the fear of what he might do if she did speak up still lingered. She pressed her lips into a thin line. "What of your father? Don't you speak to him?" He asked.

"He lost his mind a long time ago and rarely remembers who I am most of the time."

"It seems we are kindred spirits then - with only the two troublemakers to keep us company."

One of the noble girls, the ones who continued to braid their hair so intricately and do their make up even though their faces were scared with pock marks, would have taken the opportunity to say something asinine like 'now we have each other' and batted their dusty eyelashes. Mattie only nodded and studied the stones passing under their feet.

"Now. What about this girl you were chasing."

"Sir?"

"The girl in the cloak. Why were you looking for her?"

"She doesn't belong here."

"And why doesn't she belong here?"

A thousand different responses flew through Mattie's mind; because she's a villager, because she there was no way she should have been able to get across to the castle, but here she was. Because was dead and now she's alive again, which should be possible. Instead she said, "She just doesn't. Any more than I do."

"Perhaps it was merely someone you did not recognize."

"I know almost everyone here. Even the wraiths."

"I find it hard to believe that. I am the King and even I do not know who all my people are."

"Well, if you came to the Great Hall and saw your people more often..." Mattie said, the words tumbling out before she could stop them. She gasped as she realized what she'd said and pressed her mask against her face, but it was too late: the words hung in the open air. Now, he would definitely take her head.

"What was that?"

"Nothing, your Highness."

"No, I distinctly heard you say something." There was still a smile gracing his lips, but his eyes were as dark and turbulent as a stormy sky. Mattie braced herself to be yelled at again. Instead he patted her hand. "That's the second time your tongue has almost gotten you in trouble. You would do well, my dear, to remember to think before you speak in my presence."

"I'm sorry, your Highness. I'll go."

"No. Stay. Please. It's been too long since I've had someone other than my men or those two to speak with – though I'm sure if I came to the Great Hall like you suggested just a few moments ago, I'd find myself someone willing to converse with... Or would they all be so startled by appearance that they would freeze up like you?"

Mattie wanted to sink into the ground or run and hide in embarrassment, but the ground was solid beneath her feet and the King's grip on her hand too strong for her to pull away politely. Instead she bowed her head. "I'm sure your people would appreciate it if they saw you more often, sir. There are rumors that you are dead or have gone mad."

"Well now you can reassure them that I am quite whole and sane."

"Yes, sir."

"I do have other names you know." He smiled down at her, his expression playful. "Some call me My Lord, others say Your Highness..."

They turned down another path that was just as eerily familiar as the one Mattie had followed into the garden. She tilted her head back, looking at the stars and moon above through the tree branches that arched overhead. Those trees would bloom with bright green leaves and pink flowers come spring time, and this pathway would stay cool throughout the summer.

She shivered, yet again wondering how she knew all of this and recognized it even though she'd never stepped foot inside of this garden before. The King pressed her hand tighter against his side. "Are you alright?"

"Yes, sir... I mean, my lord, I am fine. What is this place?"

"I thought that would be rather obvious; it's a garden."

"Yes, but none of the other gardens are this well-kept."

"None of the other gardens are my personal gardens."

"But the entire castle is yours as well, why is it not..." Mattie bit her lip. Just because he had been tolerant of her so far, didn't mean his mood would last.

However, the fury she was expecting never came. "The castle would require a whole army for me to maintain, and there are only a few of us left. This," He motioned to the plants around them with his free hand. "I can easily take care of by myself."

She nodded, but stayed silent as more memories that were not hers surfaced in her head. According to them, nearby was a small statue hidden under a bush, marking the site where a beloved pet had been buried after it passed away. The King had finally relaxed his grip on her hand enough that she could pull away from him. She did so, and wandered ahead, stopping next to a bush that was just off the path. She squatted down to see if the statue she remembered was still hidden there. A stone fawn with a faded ribbon tied around his neck gazed back at her.

"No one has ever noticed that before." The King spoke, his voice suddenly imperious again.

Mattie stood quickly and scurried away so she wasn't within the King's reach. His men, who had been following them at a distance, stepped forward, surrounding her and blocking any chance of escape. "I'm sorry, I..."

His voice snapped though the frigid air. "Stop apologizing."

"Yes, sir..." Remembering that he wanted her to call him something else, she quickly added. "I mean, your highness."

"Who are you?"

"I told you, sir. I'm Mattie. The Toymaker's daughter."

"How did you know that that was there?"

"I don't know."

"Lies." The lips that smiled at her so kindly earlier were now twisted into a cruel sneer. "How can you not recall remembering something?"

"I don't know." She repeated. "I don't remember much from before the curse - I only know what Rordan and Talesin told me."

"Then how did you know that the fawn was there?"

"I saw it through the leaves." She lied, and she immediately regretted it. From where she currently stood it was clear that she would not have been able to see the white of the stone statue through the thick leaves of the bush it was hidden underneath.

A slower person might have bought it, but the King was anything but slow. "Try again."

Mattie licked her lips nervously, glad once again that her mask hid her fear from him. "They said that the Queen favored my father."

"She did; she was always ordering some new toy or gift from him so we would be ready for..." He trailed off and looked away, his hands clenching and unclenching into fists.

So, Mattie thought, the nursery she had come across earlier was a royal one after all. "Maybe I was allowed to play here when they met."

"She was found of children." He admitted, though he continued to regard her with suspicion. "Normally merchants do not bring their progeny with them to audiences regarding business matters - however, I must admit, your father was hardly one for protocol, so it is possible that she may have allowed you to play here while they spoke."

"That must be it then, your highness."

"Do you remember her at all?"

"No." She stammered and then corrected herself, when an image of a pale woman with dark hair flashed across her mind. "I don't know. Maybe. Did she have black hair? Light eyes?"

"Yes. Come." The King didn't touch her this time, but motioned that she should follow him. They continued down the path until they reached a circular clearing that Mattie didn't recognize. She closed her eyes for a moment and sighed in relief, happy to finally be someplace that was not plagued with memories that were not her own.

However, her reprieve did not last long; the King pushed past her and walked over to where a statue of a woman in stately robes stood in the middle of the clearing. A ring of rose bushes surrounded its base, the vibrant red blooms filling the air with a pleasant scent. He stepped between two of them and leaned down to dust a stray leaf off the statue's foot. "This was what my wife would have looked like at the time you might have known her. In life, her hair was as dark as yours and her eyes were grey - also like yours."

"Oh."

"In fact, you remind me of her - except for your damned mask. She never would have worn something so silly."

"In life? Is she..." Mattie asked. Were the rumors true then? Had something happened to the Queen after all? "I thought she disappeared."

"Yes."

"Yes, she's dead or...?"

The King stepped out of the rose bushes and came to stand in front of her. He stared at her silently for a moment or two, and Mattie gulped. He hadn't yet thrown her to his men, but surely now he would. She should have stayed in the library and ignored the girl, if she had not followed her, she would not be in the mess she was currently in. "I am the one asking the questions here."

"Yes, sir. Sorry, sir."

"But yes, she is dead. We were unable to find a body though since she threw herself off the waterfall. While we can survive falling great heights thanks to this... curse... I doubt she would have been able to survive the rapids. The rocks there would have torn her to pieces."

Mattie nodded and looked up at the stone face staring down at them. Something about it tickled her memory even more the garden she was walking through, but she couldn't understand why it did any more than she could explain her familiarity with her surroundings. Perhaps the guess she made about meeting the Queen was true after all. Perhaps her father had brought her with him once or twice and the Queen had let her run around the garden while they discussed business. Yes, she seized on the idea, that had to be how she knew this place.

"It's a pity; she was well loved by all." The King continued to speak. Mattie nodded numbly, but it was clear he expected more from her. When she did not say anything, he turned away from her. "You may go now."

"Your highness?" She asked, surprised that she was being let go so easily.

"Julius will escort you to the Great Hall."

"Yes, your Highness." She bowed – not that he noticed, for he was still staring at the statue of his wife – as one of his men, an imposing figure dressed in leather and mail, stepped forward and grabbed her arm. He pulled her along roughly, dragging her back down the path and out of the garden. Mattie struggled to keep up with his longer gait.

"You're going too fast." She complained after she stumbled and was jerked to her feet for the third time in as many steps.

The guard, Julius, released her arm with a grunt. "Do you know how to get back to the Great Hall from here?"

Mattie straightened her mask and glanced around. They were inside the castle now; standing in one of the corridors that she had ran down while chasing the girl in the cape. Doors lined the walls, and beyond them she could see rooms filled with expensive furniture. Again, she was filled with a sense of familiarity even though, like the garden, she could swear that she had never seen them until now. Was it because she had wandered these halls as a child?

The guard bent down so they were face to face and glared down at her from eyes that were glazed over with white but could still see. "Did you not hear what I just asked you?"

"No, sir - Sorry, sir."

"Do you know how to get back to the Great Hall from here?" He repeated himself, what was left of his teeth grating together as he spoke.

Mattie nodded, "Yes."

"Then go – and do not come back here again."

Chapter Nine

"What's this?" Liam's mother asked, breaking his concentration. He cursed and screwed his eyes shut but images of numbers danced across the backs of his eyelids.

"What's what?" He returned the question, and opened his eyes once more. He could do this. All he had to do was stay focused.

Keeping the books for the family store had always been Letty's job as she had a mind for numbers. Whenever he attempted to help out in the past, the numbers would change and shift on him, and they would never add up properly. It didn't matter how many times he double and triple checked his work, the tallies were always off. But since Letty was missing, and his father wasn't here, that left them with no choice. He had to handle the books himself. And he was determined that he would get it right this time.

"This... thing." She shoved a straw cross inside a braided circle under his nose.

"Oh." He sighed. So much for staying focused. "That. Old Marley gave it to me."

To his surprise, she did not smack him for calling Marley old. Instead she simply asked, "Why?"

"He said it was for protection."

"Why would we need protection? Surely they don't think she was taken by..." Her voice drifted off, unable to give sound to the names the demons who supposedly haunted the forest around their town were called. "...Them."

Liam looked up at her to find her worrying her lip between her teeth, her eyes gazing off into the distance. It was easy to see where Letty got her beauty from; according to old widows, Noya Mercat had been quite an attractive woman in her youth, attracting suitors from far and wide. There was more silver than copper in her hair nowadays, and the laugh lines around her eyes had turned into deep wrinkles, but, in Liam's opinion, she was still the handsomest woman in Mill-On-Rye.

"Of course, he does. The whole lot of them do. Fools."

That earned him a smack with her fan. "Show some respect. They may be superstitious, but they buy our things and their gold allows us to live comfortably."

"Yes, Mother." Liam rubbed at the back of his head.

"Is Marley afraid that whoever took her will come back?" Noya asked a moment later.

"He's afraid that someone followed me home from the castle."

His mother stared at him, her blue eyes wide and pale in the dim glow of the candlelight. "You went to the castle?"

"Letty loved the stories Grandpa used to tell us. She went out there every chance she got. It seems only logical that she might go there to hide."

"That stupid old man, filling her head with those tales. If she's... If they..." Noya sank down into a chair next to the desk and shook her head. Her tone turned desperate as she pleaded with him. "Don't go back there, swear to me you won't."

"Surely you don't believe in those old superstitions?" Liam asked, more than a little surprised. His mother always seemed to so practical, never gossiping like some of the other women in the village did.

"No, no, of course not." His mother replied, but there was no conviction behind the words and her eyes had that distant look in them once again. Upon noticing that he was still watching her, she sighed. "There may, or may not be, some truth behind the old legends. But do I believe that there are monsters that can't be killed hiding in the woods? No. Men with evil thoughts in their hearts? Possibly. But no monsters." She idly spun the straw charm around in her hands, stroking the ends with her finger tips.

They sat in silence for a moment as Liam checked his figures yet again. They still did not add up. "God's teeth!" He cursed, crumpling the piece of parchment up and throwing it across the room. Why couldn't he get this right? He leaned back in his chair, and scowled at the book in front of him. His mother cleared her throat, reminding him of her presence. Liam flushed. "Sorry."

The smack he was expecting for taking the Lord's name in vain never came. Instead she patted his hand absently. "It's all right dear. You have your father's temper."

He snorted. Yes, he had a temper, but it was nothing compared to his father's. If only he could make his parents understand how the words and numbers jumped around on the page! However, any time he tried to explain, they looked at him as if he were mad and insisted that he needed to try harder.

An unusual shadow falling across the desk in front of him distracted him from his thoughts. He twisted around in his chair to stare at the only window in the room - a small one located in the wall behind him. For a second he thought he saw a ghoulish face peering in at them, but when he blinked, the figure was gone.

"What is it?" Noya asked, looking from Liam's worried face with its furrowed brow to the empty window.

"I thought I saw..." He shook his head. "It's nothing."

She stood. "Perhaps you should go to bed, it's rather late."

"Yes. Good night, Mother." He called out, and then looked back at the window and frowned - but it remained empty.

His mother was right, he should get some sleep - all this talk of Undying Ones and other monsters was beginning to get to him. The shop would be closed tomorrow for the sabbath, and he had every intention of using his free time after church to return to the old bridge. He didn't know how he would cross the ravine without his grappling hook, but there had to be a way. His mother would be angry at him for breaking the commandments, however it would be worth it when he found Letty alive.

Liam shut the book in front of him and stood, stretching his arms above his head. He blew out the candle and glanced at the window one last time, expecting the figure to return now that the light was out, but all he could see was the street beyond, lined by houses like soldiers waiting to march off to battle.

Liam's dreams were filled with men bearing mutilated visages. They held Letty captive on the other side of the old bridge, and taunted him, daring him to cross. His sister struggled to break free of their grasp and cried out to him for help. Her once beautiful hair was matted, and her cheeks were stained with tears.

No matter how hard Liam tried, he could not get across the old bridge. The ravine was too steep, and the river at its bottom was too strong. The ropes in his hands weren't long enough, and when he tied them together his knots wouldn't hold. He growled in frustration.

On the other side, a woman with a white face appeared out of the mist.

"Help her! Stop them!" He called out to her, begging her to do something.

The woman answered him with silence.

And then, quite suddenly, Letty was gone. The ghouls were gone. Only the white-faced woman and the stupid old bridge remained. He looked around him in confusion, but a mist was spilling through the woods, and it was growing thicker every second. "Where...? Did she...? Letty!" He cried. "Bring her back! Bring her back now!"

"Don't yell!" His sisters voice whispered in his ear. She hugged him from behind, her ice-cold hands slipping around his middle. "I'm right here."

"Letty?" He asked and turned to face her. However, the woman standing in front of him was not the sister he remembered. The sister he loved so dearly was gone - replaced by a monster like what he had seen in the window earlier. Her beautiful face was crisscrossed with deep cuts that still bled, and she was missing part of an ear and one eye. The smell of death and decay clung to her skin, and his stomach threatened to give up its contents at the sight of her.

"No." He whispered, closing his eyes in despair. "No."

"Why do you turn away, brother?" She asked, her head cocked to one side. Clumps of her copper hair fell from her scalp and pooled around her feet like ribbons.

"Because, you're... dead."

Letty laughed. "No, dear brother, I am very much alive and very, very happy. I get to live forever, and there's no one here to tell me what to do or who to marry."

"Letty, please! Mother and father miss you. They're worried sick. We've been searching for you for weeks."

But she wouldn't listen. Instead she held out her hands to him. "Join me."

Liam shook his head. "No."

She dropped her hands, and they closed into fists at her sides. Her nails bit into the palms of her hands, dripping black blood on the ground next to the clumps of copper hair. "Then burn."

"What?"

"There's a fire coming, Liam." She warned him as she began to fade from sight. "You better run before it consumes you."

What madness was she talking about? There was no fire. No smoke or ash hung in the air. He glanced around him, calling out her name, asking, no, begging her to come back. However, only silence answered him, and the forest around him was empty of life.

The moon overhead was set quickly, leaving him in darkness so thick that he could not see his hand in front of his face. As his eyes adjusted, he noticed that there was an odd glow far off in the distance. It drew closer, it's light flickering like a candle flame, and the mist surrounding him carried the acrid scent of burnt wood.

"Fire!" Voices shouted somewhere far off and a bell sounded an alarm, it's quick peals echoing through the air. "Fire!"

The odd glow was closer now, close enough that he could feel the heat radiating off it. Embers drifted on the breeze, winking in and out of existence like firebugs.

A hand reached out of the smoke and touched his shoulder. "Liam! Wake up!" His mother's voice pleaded with him. "There's a fire at Marley's!"

Liam sat up in bed, and blinked at the rough wooden walls of his room. "What happened to the forest?" He asked, mumbling sleepily. "Letty..."

"What nonsense are you babbling about? Letty is gone." Noya threw a shirt and his boots at him. "Marley's barn is on fire. Hurry! If it spreads, we'll all be out in the cold."

Fire? Still muzzy headed, he glanced out the window as he dressed. What his mother said was true; Old Marley's barn was indeed on flames. Yellow flames lit the night sky as villagers young and old ran towards it. Some carried burlap sacks, and axes, while others hauled buckets of water from the town well.

Liam felt his mouth go dry as Letty's words from his dream came back to him. She had said that there was a fire coming, and that it would consume him. Was this the fire she spoke of, or had the smell of the smoke simply filled his dreams and twisted them?

"Liam!" Noya called, exasperated.

"Yes! Coming!" He shouted as he pulled on his boots. He followed her down the stairs and out into the street, joining the crowd that rushed to save the old barn, and their town, from burning to the ground.

The villagers fought the flames until the sun began to rise and turn the sky first a pale purple, then a dark blue, and finally orange with its light. They poured water on the flames and beat at them with dampened cloth, causing great puffs of smoke to rise in the sky. The flames continued to burn on, creeping towards the shingle roof despite their best attempts to stop it, and charring the ancient wood black and grey.

When it became apparent that they couldn't stop the fire from destroying the barn, they made sure the buildings closest to the barn were wet to prevent it from spreading. They also hacked at the beams with their axes to make sure that, when the barn eventually collapsed, it did so away from the rest of the village instead of falling on a house.

And collapse it finally did. It crashed inward on itself, sending up a shower of sparks in its wake that thankfully did not land on anyone else's house. The men fighting the blaze stepped back at that point, letting the fire eat away at what remained of the ancient wood.

Once the flames finally died down, a couple of men poured water on it until all that was left was a muddy pile of ash and burnt wood. They crept through the ruins, poking at this suspicious steaming pile or that one with their axes and shovels until they were positive that the fire was finally out.

Old Marley wandered through the yard, eyeing what was left of his barn. He leaned heavily on his cane and thanked those who had come out to help him. Many were too tired to respond; instead they merely smiled back at the man, their smiles white against their soot covered skin.

Liam leaned against a wall of a nearby house. He longed for his bed, but knew that he would need to bathe before his mother let him anywhere near the house. Judging from the reflection he'd seen in a bucket full of water nearby, his hair was grey with ash, and his skin hadn't faired any better. He also knew he reeked of smoke. They all did. It clung to their clothing and lingered in the air around them.

Marley winked at him when he passed, "Looks like I should've kept that charm for myself, eh? Perhaps it would've stopped all this..."

Liam shook his head. "A bit of straw wouldn't have stopped the flames."

"Ah, but it might have stopped those who started it." He spat on the ground. "It seems that I was right, and they followed you back."

One or two villagers who rested nearby turned and looked at them in surprise. Great, now all of Mill-On-Rye would think the fire had been his fault.

"Nonsense. The Undying Ones are an old wives' tale." Liam said, plastering a cheerful smile on his face as if he hadn't a care in the world. "They aren't real."

The villagers raised their eyebrows, but did not say anything, instead they turned to each other and began talking in whispers. Liam sighed.

"Oh, they're real all right." Old Marley continued, oblivious to Liam's discomfort. "Didn't I tell you that before?"

"Yes, sir, but..."

"Well, I saw them last night, out here, sniffing around. They're demons, they are. Always stirring up trouble."

"But if they exist, and they followed me back here, why wasn't it our barn that was burned to the ground? Or our food that went missing?"

"They aren't fools. Legend is that that king of theirs ruled over half the country, and that his men were often hired out to fight in other wars. Perhaps it was a distraction so they could cause some other mischief without us being there to stop it."

"Like?"

The old man shrugged. "Damned if I know. But they were here. I know they were. I saw them."

"Kyra, Tupper's daughter, says she saw them creeping through their garden earlier tonight." One of the villagers spoke up.

"Yeah," The man sitting next to him added. "Tupper's wife said the poor girl was scared witless."

"When?" Marley asked.

"That was... oooh... about an hour or so before the barn caught fire, I'd say." The first villager looked at his friend for confirmation.

"Yeah, that's about right." The other man nodded.

Liam remembered the shadow and the face in the window that he had seen the night before. Was it possible that they weren't figments of his imagination like he thought? He rubbed at his face with his hands, smearing the soot and ash into streaks. Damn Undying Ones. Damn gossip mongers, eager for anything scandalous. Damn Letty for running away. Damn Fire.

"Are you alright, young Liam?" Marley asked, a concerned frown causing his brow to wrinkle.

"Yes. Fine." He lied. "We'll get together and build you a new barn soon." He found himself promising, in a desperate attempt to turn the conversation away from the Undying Ones. "We'll donate the nails if someone can gather the lumber"

"That's nice of the Mercat clan to offer, but don't worry about it." Marley clapped him on the shoulder. "I haven't needed or used a barn in years. In fact, I should've torn down ages ago."

"You'll need someplace to store your wood and food for the winter..."

"There's a kitchen for the food, and a lean to for wood. All I need is a spry young man to help me out with stocking it."

"I..." Liam stammered. It would look good if he helped, but at the same time, spending time helping Old Marley would take time away from his search for Letty.

Marley laughed, "Don't worry about it - I know you have more important things to worry about. Now, go home and get some rest, boy."

"Yes, sir." Liam nodded and pulled himself away from the wall. He waved to his mother, motioning back up the road towards the house. She nodded in understanding, then returned to handing out coffee to the exhausted firefighters with the other women of Mill-On-Rye. She seemed oblivious to how they stared at her or whispered behind her back, but Liam could see the strain in the smile on her face. He hoped she would follow his lead and return home soon, but he knew would remain until everyone was taken care of.

The streets through the village were thick with mud from all the water that had been carried between the well and Marley's barn. It sucked at Liam's boots as he walked, and once or twice he almost lost one to the muck, but he finally reached the safety of their home.

Remembering what Marley said about the fire possibly being a distraction, Liam found himself eyeing the front of the store. Everything appeared to be just as they left it; the windows shone in the early morning sun, and the porch was still clean from when he had swept it last night.

He stripped to his waist, and washed off the soot from the fire as best as he could using the water from the rain barrel sitting under the eaves. It was icy cold, and made his teeth chatter and his skin break out in gooseflesh, but pulling the tub from the pantry would take too long - especially when all he wanted to do was crawl back into bed and sleep.

Once he felt he was clean enough, he pulled off his boots and stepped onto the porch. The door swung open at his touch. He froze struggling to remember if his mother had locked it, or if she had forgotten in the rush to stop the fire. Regardless, nothing seemed to be missing from the shelves, or from the kitchen just behind the store.

He shook his head, laughing at himself; Old Marley's talk about the Undying Ones was beginning to get to him. "It's not real, remember?" He told himself as he took the steps upstairs two at a time. "Just an old wives' tale."

However, when he reached the threshold of his bedroom, he froze. Hanging in the doorway was the grappling hook he used in his attempt to cross the gorge. At least he assumed it was his grappling hook - the thing was so damaged it was hard to tell exactly. The prongs were bent back against the axis and twisted around each other. Those that weren't had been broken off, leaving gagged metal holes in their place.

And tied to it was a page torn out of the accounts book he'd been working on the night before, with a warning to stay away from the castle written in thick black ink that stank of decay.

Chapter Ten

As soon as Mattie reached the safety of her room, she latched the door and shoved as much furniture in front of it as she could. Since the room was sparsely furnished, the barrier only consisted of her bed, chair, and table, and it would not last long if the King changed his mind and sent his men after her. She found the heaviest stones that had fallen into the fireplace and added them to the pile of furniture. She doubted that it would hold up under an attack, but it was better than nothing.

Sighing to herself, she found her piece of charred wood and made another mark on the wall. "My name is Mattie. I am a hundred years, two months and fourteen days old." She murmured to herself. Normally the words were soothing, but tonight, after all that had happened over the past couple of nights, they did nothing to comfort her. "I am the only child of the Toymaker. My father was a favorite of the Queen.

"The Queen is gone," Mattie sat down with her back against the wall. "But the King still lives... I met him tonight. I came across his garden and we... talked."

What would Talesin and Rordan say when she told them that? That she'd seen the King. That she had spoken to him, and most importantly, that he had told her that they had been lying to her all these years. That she knew they were really Lords, and belonged in the towers with the other nobles. Would they believe her? Or would they tell her that she was imagining things again?

"I remembered things about his garden that I shouldn't have. I upset him. And I'm afraid that he might send his men after me." She stared the door she had blockaded, wrapped her cloak tighter about herself, and prayed that they would not come. "And I still don't know what happened to the girl with the red hair."

Mattie spent the rest of that night, and the next huddled in her room, holding her breath every time she heard footsteps in the corridor outside her door. Most of the time it was just the whisper of slippers or leather soles, but there was the occasional well measured stomp of boots. The sound of wooden heels striking the stone floor rang through the cold halls like the peals of a death knell. Her death knell.

When she heard them, she would cower in the corner farthest from the door, convinced that it was the King's guard finally coming to drag her away. She could not die, but that wouldn't stop them from carrying her off and torturing her until she was as broken and twisted as her father.

But they never broke through the door.

Instead they faded away, leaving her shaking and exhausted until she finally gave in and slept.

On the third day, her stomach growled and cramped, reminding her that she had not eaten since she imprisoned herself. While the thought of trying to stomach more of the thin grey gruel available in the great hall was unappealing, she knew that if she didn't want to become gaunt like some of the ghouls that wandered about the castle, she needed to eat soon. At the very least, it would tide her over until she could find something better to eat. Surely there would be more berries along the bushes near the ravine. She'd spotted some there the night she broke her mask, but they had been too green to eat at the time. Perhaps by now they would finally be ready.

Sighing, she pulled herself away from the wall, her joints creaking and her muscles protesting after sitting for so long in one place. She groaned in pain as she started dragging the furniture and rocks away from the door, but her body quickly loosened up with the exertion.

Once she could open the door, she peered into the corridor outside. She glanced up and down it, looking for men wearing red uniforms and chain mail, but it was empty and the only movement she saw was the fire dancing in the torches hanging on the walls.

Breathing a sigh of relief, she shut her door firmly behind her and began her trek to the Great Hall.

However, as she drew near it, she noticed that the light spilling out into the corridor was brighter than normal. When she peered around the corner into the room, she saw that the tables were fuller than usual, and everyone had trenchers and bowls overflowing with thick stew. They chatted amongst themselves, the sound of their voices rising and falling, and even though there were guards along the walls, watching their every move, one or two brave souls were even laughing and smiling.

The crone spotted her from her spot near the large cauldron and waved at her. Mattie's stomach growled and rumbled at the prospect of food, real food, but she shook her head no. She didn't dare go near the guards after what happened in the King's garden. She quickly turned and retreated the way she had come, glancing behind her often to make sure she wasn't being followed by men in red doublets.

"Look, she does live after all!" Talesin crowed as Mattie turned a corner and almost ran into him and his brother. She went to push past them but he grabbed her arm, stopping her. "No 'hello'? No 'I've missed you my best and only friend'?"

"Some friend you are! You lied to me! You've been lying the whole time!" She shoved him hard and he fell back in surprise.

Talesin and Rordan shared a concerned look. Rordan licked what was left of his lips nervously. "Mattie, what are you going on about?"

"I met the King."

"When?" Talesin asked.

"Two nights ago."

"Where? The King hasn't left his chambers in..."

"Ages." Rordan finished for his brother.

"In his garden." She explained.

"But his garden is heavily guarded." Rordan frowned. "How did you get past his men?"

"I don't know. I was following the girl--"

"What girl?"

"The one from my father's workshop-"

"Mattie." Talesin sighed, cutting her off.

She glared at him. "She's real. I'm not mad and I'm not imagining her. I saw her--"

"But you said she was dead."

"Well, she isn't dead any longer. She's up and moving about now."

"You can't be dead and then just get up and move around... That's not possible."

None of them had any room to talk about what was and wasn't possible. Mattie raised an eyebrow at him, not that he could see it as it was hidden behind her mask. "Maybe she's been cursed too."

"The witch who did this is long gone!"

"So? Maybe the curse is in the air, or in the water, or--"

"Alright. Alright." Rordan murmured soothingly. "So, the dead girl is walking. You saw her and then... what?"

"I followed her. One minute we were in the library, the next we were in a garden." Her skin broke out in gooseflesh as she remembered the eerie feeling in the garden. How everything had been so familiar. "Then she was gone and there he was!"

"And what did you think of our King?"

"He was better looking than I was expecting."

"Well, he locked himself up in his tower when the plague hit." Talesin said. "Wouldn't let anyone come near him."

"Oh." That explained why he wasn't as scarred as the rest of them.

"And?"

"And what?"

"What happened to the Crone?"

"The King probably set his men on her." Talesin wrapped an arm around her shoulders. "Come, I hear the stew in the Great Hall is especially wonderful tonight --"

Mattie ducked out from underneath his embrace. "No! There's more; he said that you were lords!"

She watched them as the words spilled past her lips. During her time locked in her room she had prayed that the King was lying - that he was just confused, and that the brothers would laugh it off as soon as she told them, and everything would go back to normal. Instead the two shared another look, and Mattie realized with a sinking stomach that it was true. They were lords, a part of the King's noble court. "Why would you lie about something like that?"

"It's not exactly lying if the subject just never came up." Talesin said, his voice soft.

"You could have said something!"

"What good would it have done? As you can see, our association with the King hasn't exactly done us any favors." He gestured to the scars marring his face.

Rordan coughed, and laid a hand on his brother's shoulder. "We're sorry, pet. We should have told you, but we didn't think it mattered. It's all in the past, anyways."

"We always favored the Queen, you see. We came with her from her homeland as part of her court, but then things happened..."

"What things?" Mattie asked.

Talesin sighed. "Mattie..."

"Tell me. Everyone speaks of the bad times, but no one will speak of what exactly happened. Of what the curse is. Or what she had to do with it, or where she's gone!" To her surprise, neither of them seemed shocked by her outburst. They simply looked tired, and a little sad. Did they know that she could not remember things? Had she asked them this before?

"Not here. Come." Talesin grabbed her arm again, and Rordan grabbed her other one. Trapped between them, she was forced to march back around the corner and into an empty room. Inside, Mattie sat down on a chair that had lost its padding and fancy embroidery to time, watching as Talesin checked the hallway to make sure no one was near and might eavesdrop. When he was sure that it was safe, he shut the door.

"It was an arranged marriage." He explained, plopping down in another chair. Dust rose and billowed around him in a cloud. "The Queen was young, too young, some say, and fanciful. She still believed in fairytales and thought the King would be an honorable man that would love her. But he only wanted a wife so he could have an heir."

"Did they?"

"Yes. A boy."

A wisp of one of her dreams came back to haunt her.

"First the boy and now her." The phantom servant whispered.

"Perhaps it's better that way..."

Mattie shook her head to clear her thoughts, but a cold sweat broke out across her skin. It was a coincidence. Just a coincidence. She told herself.

"The bells rang for days and days when he was born." Rordan said.

"What happened to him?"

"He died before he reached two years of age."

"Oh." That explained the nursery she'd seen, and the broken toys and furniture there.

"A few days after the funeral, she was caught in the arms of a man who was not the King. Some believe that the prince may have even been her lover's son." Rordan explained, watching her closely. "But before she could be tried for adultery, she contracted the Plague. The King was so furious that she would die before he could punish her for cuckolding him that he sought a witch, and paid the woman to save her."

"Whatever the witch did worked. She was hale and healthy the last time we saw her, but she was not herself anymore." Talesin continued the tale. "She was hungry all the time, and no food would sate her. And soon the curse spread to the rest of us."

"Somehow she escaped during the chaos. No one knows how." His brother said, though, judging from his expression, Mattie guessed that he knew exactly how. She also knew that there was no point in pressing the issue - he would never confess everything. The King's words about the brothers' fondness for secrets came back to her, and she realized, that no matter how close she thought they were, or how she begged, they would never tell her everything.

"She went missing." He finished. "Disappeared into the night."

"He said she died. That she jumped off the cliffs and was lost in the rapids at the bottom of the waterfall." Mattie repeated what the King had told her.

"It's possible." Talesin allowed.

"The guards had captured us by that point." Rordan picked at a loose thread on his pants, slowly tearing a hole in the thin fabric. "We were locked up in the dungeon and didn't know what was going on except for what they told us."

"Which were taunts more often than not." His brother added.

"How did you escape?" Mattie asked.

"The King made us choose. Would we swear our fealty to him or to her? Since she was gone we did what we needed to do to survive."

Her stomach had stopped falling; now it just felt like a dead weight trapped in her abdomen. They had betrayed the Queen, then the King; would they betray her too?

"Mattie, please believe us, we would never put you in any sort of danger – and not just because of the promise…" Talesin's tone was pleading.

"Who did you make this promise to anyways?" She cut him off.

The brothers shared a look.

"It doesn't matter," said one.

"It's in the past," said the other.

There was the sound of footsteps in the hall, but thankfully it was only the slap of bare feet against stone and not the hollow clicks of wooden bootheels. Still, they fell silent, waiting for the person to pass before they continued speaking.

Finally, Rordan cleared his throat. "Mattie," he asked, his voice soft and hesitant. "Did the King say anything else during your encounter?"

The leaden weight in her stomach suddenly dissolved into molten anger. "Why do you want to know? So, you can go reporting back to him what I think of him?"

Rordan rubbed his forehead with his hand, his fingertips smudging the dirt and irritating the broken skin. "Please, not this again."

"No, it's fine." Talesin said. "Either she trusts us or she doesn't – and she doesn't. Apparently, years of loyal friendship mean nothing anymore. C'mon, let's go and get some food before the others eat all of it." He pulled his brother up from where he was sitting and into the corridor, leaving Mattie alone in the room.

Mattie took a breath, trying to calm herself. They were right - she was overreacting again. Rordan and Talesin had been her friends for centuries. Even if they did go skulking back to the King, they had done nothing to betray her. They couldn't. They had promised.

She stood, intending to go after them, but was immediately struck by the sensation of being watched. She looked around, but she could not see much: the only light in the room came from the torches in the hallway. It was dim and constantly shifting as the drafty air blew the flames about and revealed nothing but shadows of old and broken furniture. For a moment, she thought she saw the edge of a cape, and the glint of red hair, but it was gone as quickly as it came.

Rather than attempting to chase after it, she left, closing the door tightly behind her.

Chapter Eleven

The next evening Mattie wandered the castle again. She knew doing so alone was a bad idea, but except for Rordan and Talesin, she had no other friends she could rely on. The others regarded her with distrust, though she wasn't sure why, and her father was behaving stranger than other so going to him wasn't an option. However, staying in her room was driving her mad. The charcoal marks on her walls taunted her, her words echoed through the empty stone walls.

So, she sought solace in the library.

She was careful to avoid the guards, rising early before they began their patrols, and stayed late into the morning, after everyone was asleep. She darted from shadow to shadow, the sunlight nipping at her heels, but in the end it was worth it. Reading the books opened up whole new worlds for her, worlds where there wasn't any madness, or hunger, or cruelty. They told her stories about faraway lands that were made up of vast deserts. Forests larger and vaster than the one beyond the ravine. Cities full of people who didn't try to claw each other's faces off. Instead they had dances and got married and lived happily ever after.

She flipped through the old pages, the dust falling away as her breath washed over the words. Her hunger was forgotten as the stories unfolded. Sometimes she even became so absorbed in the tales, that she lost track of what was happening around her. As a result, she was nearly discovered once or twice by members of the guards. She started hiding herself deeper and deeper in the library, until she sat in the furthest corner of the room, hidden by several tall shelves, with her favorite books piled around her.

That was where she was sitting when she heard the footsteps.

They were soft at first. A whisper of leather soles against the marble floors that sounded almost like breathing. It was probably another member of the nobility, someone with an injured foot based on how every other step seemed to drag. A lady, if she had to guess, for the footsteps weren't heavy enough to be the boots of the guards. She'd spotted one or two during her evenings here - though they were often too focused on other things to notice her. They liked to come here and linger in the hopes of spotting the King, posing carefully on this ruined chair or that settee. The King never left his tower or the garden though, so they usually passed on after an hour or two.

However, rather than pausing in the middle of the library where all the chairs and tables where, these steps were drawing closer and closer.

Strange. No one ever came this deep into the library before. The ladies couldn't be bothered, and the guards were too lazy to really care. She kept expecting them to stop and turn away, but shuffle step by shuffle step, the person came nearer and nearer.

Mattie hunkered down in her hiding spot and blew out her candle. She hated to lose the dim light, especially since it had been so difficult to start, but she couldn't risk being spotted. She reached up and pulled her cloak tighter around her, making sure the hood covered the white porcelain of her mask. She did so just in time, because whoever it was in the library with her paused at the end of her row of shelves.

She held her breath, counting to ten silently while she waited for the footsteps to pass. After several long moments, they continued on. She exhaled softly and slowly, her breath steaming up the inside of her mask.

There was a thunk followed by a drawn-out creak that made Mattie's hair stand on end. She looked up just in time to see a cloaked figure with copper hair disappearing through a dark doorway that hadn't been there before.

Mattie leapt to her feet. The living doll her father made - it had to be her! She was on the move again! Surely now Rordan and Talesin would believe her. If she could find them that was. If they would even talk to her once she found them. And knowing her luck, once she found them, and convinced them to follow her back here, the doll would be gone.

But the last time she followed the figure with copper hair, she had landed up in the King's garden, and had nearly lost her head to his men. Did she dare risk that again?

She glanced towards the main entrance to the library and chewed on her lower lip, nibbling at the thin dry skin. Finally making up her mind, she decided to follow the red cloaked figure through the hole in the wall.

The corridor beyond was one that Mattie was not familiar with, and judging from the state of decay.

While it was not collapsing like other parts of the castle, the floor was covered in a thick layer of dust that was broken only by the footprints of someone wearing heavy boots. The torches on the walls put off more smoke than light due to their age, and cobwebs hung from the ceiling. They swirled and danced in the air as she passed, trailing across her hair like the fingers of ghosts.

Ahead of her, the figure with the copper hair turned around a corner, her cloak billowing out behind her. Mattie waited a moment, allowing the girl to put enough distance between them that she hopefully wouldn't notice she had a stalker, and then followed. She continued to keep enough space between them that she was still just within eyesight, but not so close that she couldn't duck into a niche if she needed too. Though, she noted as they continued to follow the corridor deeper into the castle, there weren't many nooks or crannies for her to hide in. And, aside from the turn they'd made earlier, the corridor was depressingly straight. So, if the girl with the cloak did turn around, there was nowhere for her to hide.

But the girl either didn't notice that she was being follower, or she just didn't care. She kept walking, shuffle step after shuffle step, completely oblivious to her surroundings.

The corridor finally ended abruptly at another doorway. Beyond there appeared to be a wide room with a low ceiling that was glowing with light. Mattie caught a glimpse of a table, with something long and bumpy laying on it.

For a moment, she flashed back to the night that she had found the copper haired girl in her father's workshop, and her mouth went dry. Her heart went still, freezing in her chest.

The girl had stopped.

And the girl was looking right at her.

Mattie was used to being surrounded by monsters. It was part of the curse. But the change in Marionette's appearance was shocking. Since that night in her father's workshop, her beauty had begun to fade significantly. Her perfect skin was turning sallow, and dark purple circles hung under her pale white eyes. The neat black stitches that the toymaker had made across her arms were beginning to tear through her skin. Her hair, however, was still perfect - the tight ringlets hanging around her head like a copper crown.

"You'll see him soon." She spoke, her voice crackling like dried leaves being crunched against the cobblestones of the courtyard. "Tell him not to come. Tell him not to follow. Only death lies this way." And then, her message delivered, she turned towards the right and disappeared out of sight.

Mattie rushed forward, wanting to ask who Marionette was referring to, but when she crossed the threshold, she discovered that the room was empty. All that was there was just her, the lump on the table, the toymaker's tools, and cages - so many, many, rusty metal cages.

Her chest heaving to suck in air that she didn't need, she peered into the cages, looking for any sign of the red cloak. However, the only thing they contained was a bit of straw, and a forlorn skeleton or two that no longer had the muscle or sinew to move. She started to press against the stones in the wall and tug on the torches, looking for a secret entrance out of the room. After all, if there was one in the library, surely there was another one out of here. Where else could Marionette gone?

But if there was a passage, the walls would not give up their secret. Mattie slumped against the cold stone, feeling defeated. She must really be going mad now. It was one thing to have visions and memories that weren't hers - it was quite another thing to have them deliver prophecy.

She didn't have long to bemoan her fate though - far away she heard footsteps and voices traveling towards her down the corridor. Judging from the timbre of the voices, and the heavy thunk of their feet against the stone floors, it was probably two of the King's guards.

Without the King here to call them off, the chances that they would go easy on her trespassing again were very slim. Unfortunately, there was no way she could dart past them in the narrow corridor, and since there wasn't another secret passageway, escaping that way wasn't an option. She eyed the table, but the blanket laying over the still form wasn't long enough to hide her from view.

The only option was the cages.

She chose the one that was furthest from the door, in a dark corner of the room, and quickly hid inside. Once again, she found herself pulling her hood down low over her face to hide the pale white surface of her mask and praying that whatever business they had in the room would be brief. The last thing she wanted was to be trapped in here for days on end.

However, the night wasn't finished delivering surprises just yet.

As she watched the two guards entered the room, she realized with a start that they weren't alone. Traveling in their wake was the frail figure of the Toymaker. While he had always towered over her, he was miniscule next to the giant forms of the guards. He trembled as he leaned on his walking stick, his knobby fingers clutching at its rough handle. But as she looked on, he straightened up to his full height, which, while still not as tall as the guards, was nothing to sneer at either, and the fine tremors fell away like an old coat.

He lifted an edge of the blanket and sneered. "This is what you have brought me to work with? I asked for fine specimens, not carrion."

"We were specifically told by our master to ignore your request for better quality corpses until you can provide better proof that you can deliver on your promises." One of the guards grumbled a reply.

"Was he not happy with his little doll?"

"Oh, he was happy enough," The second guard answered. His upper lip was split, and his nose was smashed against his face and the very tip shaven away. The combined effect reminded her faintly of the drawings of cats she'd seen in her books - only far more sinister. "However, she is fading fast. He wants something more permanent."

Mattie's ears perked up at that. Obviously, the doll they were referring to was Marionette. But who was him? The King? She found that hard to believe. He seemed oblivious when she mentioned the girl in the cloak the day she stumbled across his garden. But no one else had the authority in the castle, unless the guards were acting autonomously.

"I am trying my best."

"Try harder."

"This could all be solved if you would stop dragging your feet and find her." The toymaker hissed. He stepped away from the table and over to his work bench. He picked up one tool, inspected it, only to toss it aside in favor of another. However, he apparently decided that one, and the two more he picked up after it, were not what he was looking for. Finally, he settled on a short knife with a thin handle. It was dull and rusty, but the edge was still sharp and it gleamed in the candle light.

One corner of the beast guard's lip twitched upwards - not in a smile, but a growl. "You know that she has not been seen since the Queen went missing."

Mattie frowned, wondering who they were talking about.

"She probably leaped into the river to escape the curse she created." The first guard spoke up. Half of his face had been peeled away at some point, revealing the skull underneath. His teeth, the few of them that remained, were cracked, giving him a jagged, ghoulish smile.

"Then find her." Mattie's father replied.

"What do you think we do when we go to the other side?"

"You were ordered to look for subjects for my experiments, but judging from the bounty in the great hall recently, it's clear that you collect other things as well."

"You think we care about that scum?" The beast guard laughed. "The only thing they're useful for is target practice."

"Someone must." The toymaker peeled back the sheet to reveal the body of a pig laying underneath. Mattie heaved a sigh of relief that it wasn't something worse.

"The troublemakers." Skullface replied.

"Who?"

"Those two foolish brothers of the Queen's that are always sneaking about with your addle-brained daughter."

The toymaker's blade trembled in his hands and his tone turned querulous. "Daughter? I have no daughter."

The two guards shared a look, clearly they had worked with her father enough to recognize when he was starting to fade. "Yes, you do. The girl with the doll face. Remember?"

"Marionette? She is a beauty."

"No, the other one you fool." The beast guard snarled.

Skullface clapped him on the shoulder and turned to leave the room. "Leave it. You know as well as I do that there's no point in arguing with him when he's like this."

They retreated, leaving the old man to do his work.

Mattie waited until she was sure both guards were gone before moving closer to the entrance of the cage Thankfully, with her father being in the state he was in, she wouldn't need to worry about him recognizing her. However, she still found herself making sure that his back was turned to her just in case before she wiggled her way out. The finger bones of her cell mate crunched under her knees, but the toymaker was so absorbed with his work that he did not turn at the sound. Mattie breathed a sigh of relief and stood.

She continued to make sure to stay out of his sight as she slowly made her way around the edge of the room. At the front of the room there was no way to avoid it, but since he was still bent over the pig, she assumed that she would be safe. She was torn between bolting for it, and continuing her slow pace though. If she ran, he would definitely look up at the sound of her racing by, and might even follow. If she continued to creep, he might not notice her passage at all. So, she moved slowly, step by step, inching ever closer to the door and the dim corridor beyond.

Right as Mattie reached her goal, the Toymaker glanced up from his project. She froze, holding her breath and praying that he even though he was staring right at her, that he didn't actually *see* her.
Unfortunately, he did, for his eyes focused immediately on her cracked mask. However, to her immense relief, he didn't seem to recognize her at all.

"Who are you?" He asked. "And what are you doing in my workshop."

"No one." She replied. In the past, his confusion would have cut her to the core. Today, she was grateful for it. "And nothing."

He frowned, clearly puzzled, but he decided not to press the issue. He waved at her dismissively. "Well, continue on your way then."

Mattie nodded and hurried out of the room as quickly as she could without drawing any more attention to herself.

Chapter Twelve

Mattie stepped back into the library, breathing a sigh of relief as the cool damp air washed over her face. Her respite didn't last long though; she was grabbed by strong boney hands and flung to the hard ground. She slid backwards across the smooth tile floor, her mask knocked askew from the force of the fall. Quickly rolling onto all fours, she attempted to scurry away from the attack - only to run into a pair of boots standing a short distance away. They were rough to the touch, scuffed from decades of use. She looked up, her eyes taking in the worn pants and patchy doublet, until she came face to face with the beast guard from the hidden room.

His nose twitched as he glowered down at her. "I thought I smelled fresh meat."

Mattie gulped, so much for avoiding the guards notice for so long. "I'm sorry. I don't know what you are talking about. I was in the corner reading— "

"Bull shit." The Skull faced guard pulled her roughly to her feet and swung her around to face him.

"Do you know how long I've been waiting to get my hands on you?"

She knew it was a rhetorical question, but she found herself shaking her head anyways and whispering that she didn't. She wasn't a mind reader after all, but she kept her lips shut rather than let that last bit slip past them.

"Those idiots were always in the way. But they're not here anymore, are they?" He leaned close, and she could smell his moldy musty breath on her face.

"No, but I am." A new voice joined the fray.

Skullface growled at the interruption and turned to face the intruder. Then, for the second time that evening, Mattie found herself being thrown to the ground. The guards who had cornered her were bowing with their heads pressed against the floor. After seeing who was standing there, she quickly did the same thing.

"Well, this is quite a surprise." The King stepped past his guards and offered Mattie his hand. Even though her skin immediately started to crawl at the thought of him touching her, she couldn't refuse him. He was the King after all. His word was law. She placed her hand in his, grateful for the mask that covered her face and prevented him from seeing the disgust written there, and let him pull her to her feet. "I come to refresh my private collection, and instead I find two of my best men attacking one of my beloved citizens."

"Our apologies, my lord." The beast guard spoke up. "We caught her snooping around where she wasn't supposed to be."

"How so?"

The guards exchanged a look. "Your highness. You know— "

"The library is open to everyone to visit if they wish."

The guards exchanged a second look and then dropped their gazes to the floor in front of them. "Yes, sir."

"Now go."

"But the girl— " Skullface started to speak.

"Go!" The King yelled, cutting him off. Even though his face was still the very image of perfection, a sharp contrast compared to the nightmares that lived and breathed around him, his eyes flashed with a dark fury that made everyone cower before him.

The guards quickly scattered, leaving Mattie alone with a man who equally terrified her and thrilled her at the same time. He held out his hand. She looked up at him, waiting for him to yell at her too, but the storm in his eyes was quiet for the moment.

She took his hand, letting him pull her to her feet. "Thank you, your highness."

"You're very welcome." He offered her a small smile, then cleared his throat.

Mattie quickly remembered herself. Instead of making herself prostrate at his feet like she had before, she curtseyed like the ladies in her books did. The King arched a perfect eyebrow in surprise. She blushed behind her mask. "I'm sorry. I... I'll just be going now."

"No. Stay. I don't trust them entirely - they could be lingering in the hallways. Waiting for a second chance. You'll have to be careful from now on."

"I always am."

"Obviously not." His lips quirked upwards in a smile.

Mattie felt her cheeks flush again – this time from shame instead of embarrassment. "That was my mistake. I should have waited longer."

"Mhm. May I ask what you are doing here?"

"Why do you care?" The words slipped out before she could stop them. "I'm sorry your highness. I didn't mean— "

Even though his eyes flashed with anger, he waved his hand dismissively. "No. It's quite all right. After all – I never leave my rooms so what would I care about the rest of the castle?"

"I only meant that you yourself just said that the library was free for anyone to visit. So why do you care about me being here?"

"Aside from the ladies who linger here in the hopes of attracting my attention, and the guards on patrol, no one else dares to set foot in here. I was curious what brought you here. If it was a desire to better yourself, to escape for a short period, or a hunt for food."

"Oh."

"I confess if it's the later, you'll be very disappointed. The leather was stripped from the bindings long ago, and paper doesn't taste good."

Mattie glanced at the silent tomes around them, reevaluating their use. Yes, the paper by itself would be very dry and bland, but if it was mixed with enough spices... "You'd be surprised at how creative you can be when you're hungry enough."

He chuckled, and she found her stomach flip flopped at the sonorous rumble. "I don't doubt it. Please don't mention it to the others. I'd hate to have to barricade the doors against the masses."

"My lips are sealed. Though I don't think you have to worry – the great hall has been pretty full lately."

"So, the rumors are true then? A new cache of supplies has been discovered?"

She stared at him in surprise. "Your men didn't tell you?"

"They did, but when one day runs into the next for centuries on end, you forget when things happen. I admit that some of these books are mine, filled with notes to help me keep track of time."

"You wouldn't be the first to use that trick." She thought of the ash marks that lined the walls of her room.

He smiled at her, and she felt her stomach flip flop in ways that had nothing to do with the hunger gnawing at her belly. She understood now why the noblewomen swanned about, waiting for a glimpse of him. Yes, he was devastatingly handsome, but he was also quite charming when his anger was in check.

Don't fall for it, a voice whispered deep in her mind. *He cannot be trusted. None of them can.* A flash of him standing over her, his eyes dark with fury and a snarl marring his pretty mouth crossed her memory. She flushed, though she wasn't entirely sure if it was from embarrassment at being the sole focus of his attention, or at being chastised by an imaginary voice.

"Well, since the rumors are true, and there is food to be found in the great hall, shall we attend?"

"I... um..." Mattie stammered.

"I assume you must be hungry. I can hear your stomach growling, but if you have other sustenance you'd rather enjoy..." He trailed off.

"No! No!" Remembering herself, she licked her lips and attempted to start again. "I mean, your highness, I... I appreciate your offer, and I would enjoy my... your... any food..."

When she didn't continue for a few moments, he prompted her. "...But?"

"I do not think my friends would handle it very well, if I were to arrive with you."

"Leave them to me."

"Also, I have a question my lord."

"Yes?"

"Why me?"

"Pardon me?"

"Why me?" She repeated herself and then expanded on the question once she noticed his confused look. "I'm just a lowly peasant. The daughter of the toymaker. I'm nothing much to look at. I have scars. I wear a mask. I dress in rags, not fancy gowns. Why not one of the noble daughters who are constantly vying for your attention?"

He glanced around. "I don't see anyone else around. Do you?"

That was not quite the answer that she wanted, but then she wasn't really sure what she was hoping for. He made her heart pound so loudly in her ears that she could barely hear the voice telling her to run, but that fear lingered in the shadows of her mind.

She glanced around. Other than his other guards lingering in the shadows, they were completely alone. "No."

"Besides," He added. "You intrigue me. I feel as if we've met before, though that may just be from all the stories I've heard from your friends."

"I thought they avoided you."

"I wasn't speaking of the brothers. In fact, perhaps 'friends' is too generous a name for them."

"Hm." She eyed the guards, then changed the subject back to the original topic. "I intrigue you?"

"Yes."

"Most people think I'm an irritating problem that needs to be squashed."

The King smiled, then took her hand and placed it on his arm. "I'll be the judge of that."

Chapter Thirteen

As they drew near to the Great Hall, Mattie's legs burned with the overwhelming desire to run away. To wait until the flames on the torches nothing more than faint embers and the guards were dozing at their posts before she slipped inside to eat her portion. As long as she kept her head down, no one should notice her. But she'd been keeping her head down and trying to avoid any attention all her life, and look what that had gotten her. She still managed to attract attention no matter what she did.

Besides, it wasn't as if she had a choice. The King held her hand trapped firmly in the crook of his arm, and even if she did manage to break away from him, his guards would surely stop her. And even if he wasn't escorting her, the smell of food emanating from the Great Hall was too strong for her to ignore. Even though it would do nothing to end the ever-constant hunger, her stomach growled so loudly that one or two of the guards stared at her in surprise. The King, however, politely ignored it.

Inside the Great Hall, men and women, their faces scarred and haunted, sat around tables laughing and chatting as they ate. The trenchers and bowls in front of them were piled high with roasted meat and vegetables - some of which Mattie hadn't seen in years. There was bread too! Fresh bread! And fruit! Her mouth watered at the sight of it.

A guard standing near the door banged his staff on the floor. The citizens of the castle feel silent and looked up. Their mouths fell open at the sight of the King standing in front of them. Their eyes going wide as they took in the bedraggled site of Mattie next to him.

"His highness, the King." The guard announced, his voice ringing through the silent room.

The King walked towards his dais, his boots ringing on the stone steps, and stood still for a minute before the throne, his eyes taking in the cowering citizens around him. When he finally sat, one of his guards took up a position to the right and slightly behind the King while another stood at the bottom of the dais, his muzzle turned up into a continuous snarl.

Noticing that Mattie still stood by the door, The King motioned for her to come forward. She did so, crossing the stone floors as quickly as possible. She took the steps up to the dais two at a time, and then came to a stop before him. "Yes, my lord?"

He motioned to a spot next to the throne. "Wait here."

"Yes, your highness." She stood, keeping her eyes on the ground in front of her.

Silence continued to reign in the hall, broken only by the castle citizen's panicked breathing. The King continued to glance around the room, his gaze skimming over those present. Finally, he broke the silence, "Why, is there no music?"

The question echoed through the hall, making a few gasps in surprise, but no one stood to answer. "My halls were once filled with music. Now they are silent. Where are Bonsky and Piper?"

A man with a skeletal face seemed to shake himself out of a trance when King's gaze finally fell on him. He waved a hand very briefly in the air, "Here, my lord."

"Why are you not playing?"

Mattie knew why. After the curse struck, whatever drums the man owned had been sacrificed for food. However, rather than confess that he'd eaten the skins, the man stammered, "I am sorry, my lord, but your sudden appearance..."

"Play!" The King roared, his voice so deafening that many covered their ears with their hands. Someone passed Bonsky a bucket, while someone else handed him a stick. He immediately upended it and launched into a complicated beat. Another man with a dragon carved into his cheeks stood and lifted a pipe to his lips. He struggled to keep up with Bonsky, but after a few minutes, they fell into a more harmonious rhythm.

Conversations interrupted by the King's entrance nervously started back up again while the King looked around the room, nodding at those subjects he recognized. Mattie dared to look up as well, noticing two familiar figures sitting at a table near the back of the hall. They gawked at her, their mouths hanging open as if their jaws were unhinged and their eyes wide in their scared faces. If they still had eyebrows, she was sure that they were lost somewhere in what remained of their respective hairlines. She grimaced to herself and quickly looked away - so much for avoiding the brothers.

The King touched her hand. "Why don't you go get some food for yourself?"

"Yes, sir." Mattie nodded and stepped down from the dais, hurrying towards the cauldron nearby. When she reached it, she peered inside only to discover that it was almost empty of stew, and the only bits of bread left on the table nearby were burnt. However, it was more than she'd had in weeks, so she pocketed some of the bread, and greedily scraped what she could of the stew into a nearby bowl. She licked her fingers clean, freezing when she realized the ingredients tasted fresh instead of stale and moldy.

She glanced at the tables around her, wondering where the meal had come from? And how was there so much? Supposedly the last of the castles stores had expired years ago. Were there more reserves down in the dungeon that they weren't aware of? Is that why Rordan and Talesin went through that heavy door the other day? But how was the food still fresh? Any supplies should down there should have gone bad long ago...

"I was wondering when you would finally come in." An old woman's voice cackled and Mattie turned to find the crone behind her. "Here, you'll find this much tastier than what you have."

Mattie eyed the bowl full of stew and fresh bread warily. "I'm quite fine."

"Oh, hush child. You need your strength! Take it." The crone practically pushed the food into her hands.

"But, I already have -"

"I'll take that rubbish to your father, dear. He deserves naught but scraps for the mess he's gotten himself into."

"Excuse me?" Mattie asked, feeling more than a little confused at the mention of her father – and that the crone knew who he was.

"Don't you worry your pretty little head over it." The old woman tisked, spittle flying from her dry lips. "You'll have bigger things to concern yourself with soon enough."

"What things?" She demanded.

But her questions fell on deaf ears; the crone turned her about and was pushing at her, nudging her back towards the dais. "Go."

A part of her was tempted to run for it. To find some shadows near the wall and eat her meal in peace and quiet, but the King was expecting her to return. She could feel his eyes boring into her as she climbed the steps once more and she flushed under the fierceness of his gaze.

He motioned for one of his men to bring her a stool, and directed them to place near his throne. Sighing, she sat down, tucking her legs under her in such a way that she could easily get up and run if she needed to. Rather than trying to make small talk with him, she dug into stew the Crone gave her. She sucked on each piece of meat, enjoying the flavor as the juices dripped on her tongue and down her throat. The chunks of potatoes and onions were just as savory, and the bread was rich and chewy. She hummed in delight as bit by bit, the meal disappeared into her gullet.

"You would not remember, since we very rarely allowed your class in the Hall back then," The King spoke, breaking his silence. "But things were not always like this. We used to hold balls and dinners here - nobility would come from miles around just to take part in the festivities."

Mattie looked around the room, trying to imagine what it might have been like back then, when the tapestries on the walls had been bright instead of tattered and the people at the tables around the dais where healthy and whole. Would it be strange to wear dresses instead of rags? To be proud of their faces instead of hiding them? Suddenly everything felt disjointed, and for a moment she thought she could see what the King had been talking about. She could almost feel the fancy clothes on her skin. She could see the people dancing. But it was gone as soon as quickly as it had come. She shook her head to clear her thoughts.

"Maybe, someday, we'll have that again." He continued. "Would you like to see it when we do?"

"I don't know. Will lowly peasants like me be allowed in the Hall?"

"Of course. But hopefully you won't be a peasant." She frowned up at him, grateful that her mask covered her confusion at his words. Was he implying what she thought he was?

The doors to the hall opened once again - this time with an ominous groan instead of a bang - revealing the Toymaker. Mattie gasped at the sight of her father standing tall, and without the use of a cane, for the first time in ages. He crept through the hall leading a small figure - cloaked in red - that moved very stiffly. Mattie felt as if her food might come up as she recognized her. Marionette. She glanced around the room, making sure that everyone else was seeing what she did. They gaped at the sight in front of them, and she felt a little relieved that she wasn't going mad like she thought she was. But then she made the mistake of looking back at the King, and she felt afraid again. His eyes narrowed, and his expression became cold like the stone face of the statue of the Queen in the garden.

One of the guards stepped forward from his spot near the dais, one hand on his sword. "What do you want, Toymaker?"

Her father tensed when he saw her sitting at the King's feet, but he did not call out to her. Instead he gazed at her for a long moment, then he turned to the king and licked his lips. "A word with my lord, is that too much for a lowly citizen to ask?" The Toymaker's voice was low and gruff from years of inhaling glue and sawdust though there was an underlying current of anger that Mattie had never heard before - not even during one of his mad fits. Was it because she was with the King?

The guard threw a quick look back the King. "Our lord is..."

"Let him speak." The King leaned forward in his throne. "What is it that you want to tell me, Toymaker? And what is it that you have hidden behind you?" He nodded at the person under the cloak.

"I only wish to say that today would have been her Highness, the Queen's birthday..."

One of the guards growled and the other's hand tightened on his sword hilt. The King did nothing more than frown, his eyes narrowing as he glared at the Toymaker. "I am aware of that."

"I wished to present her with a gift."

Mattie groaned to herself and bowed her head. Foolish, foolish man. She thought he would be so wrapped up in whatever project the guard had given him to bother them. Clearly whatever subjects they brought to experiment on were still not up to his snuff.

"Well, as you can see, dear Toymaker, the Queen is no longer with us." A few nervous titters broke out at the King's words and Mattie flushed under her mask.

"I am aware of that, my lord. But I continue to hold out hope that she will return to us some day."

"And what makes you think that?"

"The crone is among us. I have spotted her wandering the castle several times this week. If she can return, then it's possible that our Queen may yet come back to make things right." He glanced at Mattie as he spoke, then turned his gaze back to the King. "It seems only right that I turn this gift over to you for safe keeping until she returns." The Toymaker bowed deeply.

The King's frown deepened. "Destroy it. I have no use for whatever you might have made. I am not the flighty thing the Queen was, constantly needing entertainment from dolls and toys."

"But I'm sure you have been lonely since the Queen left, and would appreciate female company."

"I have all the company I require here." Mattie was aware of the King resting his hand on her head. She felt her heart pound in her chest at his touch. Out of the corner of her eye she saw both Talesin and Rordan pale - well as much as the dead like them could - at the King's words. "And if the Queen is bound to return, like you claim she is, then I will have her to rely on as well."

The Toymaker's smile faltered, "But I have never done finer work..."

"I. Do. Not. Care." The King growled, clipping each word off shortly.

"Humor an old man." The Toymaker said and pulled the cloak off the figure, revealing Marionette.

Mattie didn't think it was possible, but the villager had decayed even more during the brief time since she last saw her. Her eyes were sunken and flat, and the neat stitches her father used to piece her back together had pulled through the skin in some places, leaving her limbs dangling by frayed threads. Her copper curls were piled high on her head now, and the dress the Toymaker dressed her in had been barely touched by the moths. It was fit for royalty, decorated with jewels that sparkled in the candle light. Mattie wondered where he had found it, for she'd never seen anything so beautiful before.

Mattie glanced back up at the thing's face to find that the girl was watching her. For a moment, she wondered if she would speak again but instead her gaze moved away and settled on the King as if Mattie was no more than a spec of dirt.

"I give you Marionette." The Toymaker introduced the thing, breathing heavily as he stared up at the King.

The entire hall froze, waiting to see what their leader would do next. The King stared at the girl in front of him. His face was completely white as if he had seen a ghost. It took him a moment or two to recover from his shock. When he did, his voice was almost inaudible when he spoke, "What is this... this thing you have created?"

"I created a doll, as the Queen asked me to."

"From an outsider?"

"Yes."

"Does not one of my rules state that the outsiders are not to be harmed!?" The King roared making Mattie flinch in surprise.

Her father didn't waiver though. He met the King's glare and answered, "Yes."

"Then what is this!? How did she come to be here!?"

"I do not know. I found her remains in my workshop. I decided it would be wasteful to just let such a fine piece rot. So, I sewed it up, and was going to give it to the Queen, but then I remembered that she was no longer with us. I gave too much time to this poor soul to cast her away, so I decided that it would be best to continue on and give her another chance at life."

"How?"

"The same way we came to be. How else, my lord?"

"She should have been left where she was, Toymaker. What if the outsiders come looking for her? They would destroy us!"

"You know as well as I do that none can cross the ravine."

"I should have you strung up for this."

"But you won't because our numbers dwindle."

"That fact did not stop me from correcting the chef when he made his error."

Mattie clutched at the King's sleeve. "Please, your highness."

He glanced down at her, his jaw clenched, and shook his head. "Your father goes too far."

"More and more of us go missing every year, because their bodies finally give out and fade away to dust." The Toymaker's voice grew in strength as he spoke, and his eyes flashed with a clarity that Mattie hadn't seen in years. This, she thought to herself, must have been what her father was like in his youth - before the plague and the curse drove him and the rest of the world mad. "I have done nothing wrong - just given a poor soul another chance at life. A life we desperately need if we are to continue on."

"It's unnatural."

"We are unnatural, or did you forget what that spell of yours did?"

There was silence in the hall as the King glared at the Toymaker. Finally, he leaned back in his chair limply and rubbed his forehead with a hand. "Is it alive? Can it speak?"

"Yes."

"Can she think for herself?"

"She seems to."

"Well, then, let's ask her what she wants." He sat forward again and stared at the Marionette. "What is your wish, girl? Do you want to continue to live this damned life as one of us?"

"Any life is better than death." The doll's voice sounded empty and tinny. It was so totally different from the voice that she had used to deliver her warning earlier that Mattie stared at her in surprise. "Let me stay and serve you, your Highness."

"But don't you have some family that you wish to return to?"

"I have no one - just my creator."

Lies! Mattie thought, remembering the villager from the bridge and his search for the missing girl, but she did not speak. Even if Marionette wanted to return there, it was simply not possible now. They would destroy her if they saw her, and then follow her trail back to the castle.

The King continued to study the girl in silence. She stared back at him calmly, waiting for his decision. Finally, he sighed. "She can stay."

Mattie looked at him in surprise and several of the guards and survivors cried out in shock. "If we sent her back to her outsiders they will call her a monster and burn her at the stake for witchcraft." He continued, voicing the very thoughts running through Mattie's head. "She stays."

"She'll be a freak here too." One guard argued.

"Silence!" The King roared. Again, everyone in the Great Hall flinched. "As the Toymaker has reminded me yet again, we are all freaks here. This is the only sanctuary we have left."

With that he stood and left the room abruptly without so much as a backward glance at Marionette or, Mattie realized, herself.

Chapter Fourteen

Liam stood in the middle of a great stone corridor that he did not recognize. Nothing in Mill on Rye was this grand. Nor was anything in Mill on Rye was this decrepit. Carved buttresses held up the arched roof that towered overhead. Faded flags hung from them, along with long ropes of dusty cobwebs. Along one wall was a row of windows looking down on a sloping hill covered with dead trees. Most of the glass was broken out of them, but based on the fragments still stuck to the stone frames, he could guess that they had been filled with ornate stained glass once upon a time.

Far off in the darkness, a woman cried. He followed the sobs, his boot heels echoing off the rough stone walls. The girl started to wail - a heartbreaking cry that chilled him to his bones. He increased his pace and stepped through a heavy metal door. On the other side was a spiral stone staircase that went down into the bowels of the earth. He eyed the dim torches on the outside wall of the staircase, wondering how long they would last before they guttered out. A minute? Two? Three?

The wailing was louder now, broken up occasionally by dry sobs, so Liam decided to take his chances. He took the steps down two at a time. The walls grew damp the further down he went, and the stone started to be covered by a thin layer of mildew. He almost slipped a few times, but he recovered his balance by slapping his palm against the rough walls and leaning into it to steady himself.

When he pulled his hand away, he saw his skin was covered with thick black slime. He retched and quickly wiped it off on his pants. Then, after taking another breath to clear his throat of the bile that threatened to overwhelm him, he continued on - a little more carefully this time.

The stairs dropped him off in a cavernous room lined on either side by rusting metal cells. The ground was covered in a film of dark water that lapped at his ankles and in the distance, beyond the wailing, he could hear the distant roar of a waterfall. With every step, ripples spread off into the shadow to lap against the walls of the chamber. He pulled a torch off the wall to light his way. It was brighter than the ones in the stairwell, but it still couldn't quite chase the shadows from the edge of the chamber.

He finally found the source of the crying in the last cell.

Huddled on a thin plank of wood hanging from the wall with thick chains, sat a woman wearing a tattered black dress that reminded him of the fairy tales his grandfather used to tell him. It appeared to be made of fine silk and linen, and was beaded with jet glass. Her head was bowed over a bundle of rags that she held cradled in her lap. He couldn't see her face, for her dark hair hung around her like a curtain, but what little he could see through the tangled strands was pale and blotchy.

She seemed oblivious to Liam's presence. She continued to moan and cry, thick tears staining the pile of cloth in her arms. He reached out to touch her, but a familiar voice stopped him.

"Don't. If you love your life and all that you hold dear, leave her be!"

"Letty?" Liam turned to find his sister standing at the gate to the cell. She wore a faded red cape that was probably as ancient as the gown the crying woman was dressed in. The hood was pulled forward to hide her face, but he could see her copper hair peeking out from underneath its shelter. "We can't leave her here. She needs help."

"She's dead." Letty's voice was far more gravely than normal but still recognizable. "We all are."

"But..."

"Liam, please." The woman stopped her crying suddenly and Letty gasped. She reached out and grabbed his wrist. Her touch was like ice. "You need to go!"

"Why? What is it?"

"Now!"

He looked back to find that the woman was moving. She tilted her head, and brilliant blue eyes peered up at him from an ashen face. Her full lips were parted slightly as her gaze skimmed over his face and down to his throat. She sat her bundle aside and started to stand, sliding down from her perch and gliding through the water to stand in front of him.

Liam stared at her, completely stunned. Despite her ghostly appearance, she was quite beautiful.

"Liam! You need to go now!"

But it was too late, for the woman lunged up to grab him. He could feel the press of her teeth against his skin, followed by the stinging pain as they broke through the surface of his skin. His blood pulsed out of him with every beat of his heart. He cried out in shock, and pushed her away, but she was far stronger than himself. Her fingers dug into his arms, and when he attempted to kick her away, she shoved him against the wall of her cage and pinned him there. Even though a part of him knew it was futile, he continued to fight back, twisting first one way and then the other, trodding on her feet, and biting her ear - the only part of her face he could reach. Her blood filled his mouth, thick and sweet.

Through the struggle, he could hear Letty crying out to him. "I warned you."

Liam woke up gasping for air. Even though his mouth was dry, he could still taste the coppery tang of the woman's blood on his tongue. His hand flew to his neck and found that his skin was smooth and unbroken. He let out a sigh of relief, relaxing into the crunchy stiffness of the straw mattress beneath him. Once he finally managed to push the memories of the dream into the shadow of his mind, he flung the blankets that were tangled around his legs away from the bed and sat up. The room lurched around him and he leaned his head in his hands and closed eyes.

From downstairs, he could hear the maid moving around the kitchen. Normally it was the cook, a jolly woman nearing the end of her middling years, who started breakfast. However, she was visiting her daughter who delivered a baby recently, so the job had fallen to their maid. He was a little hesitant to see what slop she came up with for breakfast, as her previous attempts to cook weren't even safe for pigs to eat, but his growling stomach overruled his better judgement. The clink of the iron skillet on the stove drifted through the floorboards followed shortly by the hiss and pop of eggs frying. He could smell bacon wafting through the air of the house too - a much more welcome smell than the decay from the castle his dreams had built.

Once the room righted itself, he stood and dressed. After pulling on his boots, he took the steps down to the small living area behind the store two at a time. A vision of the stairs from the dream flashed before him, and he froze as the dank smell of mildew flooded his senses again before disappearing just as quickly as it came. He reached out and touched the wall, sighing in relief when his fingertips met rough wood instead of stone.

To his surprise, instead of the maid he found his mother bent over in front of the stove. Noya deftly shoved more wood into its dark depths, the orange glow of the flames dancing across her weary face. She stood up at the sound of his approach. "Good morning."

"Good morning." His reply was little more than a grunt as he poured ground coffee kernels into a bit of cheesecloth. He tied it into a ball, then dropped it into a wooden mug. Once that was done, he pulled a whistling kettle off the stove top and poured its contents into the mug. Within moments the aroma of spiced coffee filled the air. "You're up early."

She stole his mug before he could take a sip of the deep brown liquid it contained. "That wretched girl sent her brother to tell us that she is ill. Judging from his high-handed attitude, and the way he sneered down his nose at me as he delivered her message, I think it's more likely that her family has decided they cannot risk her precious honor by associating with us."

"Ah." Liam had noticed more whispers and sidelong looks when he walked down the street lately, but thankfully the townsfolk hadn't abandoned the store yet. Since they were the only store in Mill-on-Rye though, the townsfolk couldn't really snub them completely if they wanted to eat more than dried meat, fish, or whatever berries they could find in the woods.

"They'll see soon enough just how honorable their daughter is when her belly starts to..."

"Mother!"

Noya sighed and relinquished Liam's mug back into his care. "My apologies. While I am perfectly capable of cooking breakfast, I confess I'd much rather be in bed."

"I think we all would rather be in bed."

"You did not sleep well?"

"Nightmares."

"Hm." She rubbed her hands on her apron. "Your father sent a message."

"Oh?" Liam nursed his coffee slowly, his hands cupped around it to protect it should his mother decide to steal it again.

"There's no sign of Letty at the port, so they will be catching a ship to the mainland to search there."

"That's foolish." His words earned him a smack on the back of the head for daring to criticize his father. "Mother, she didn't take any coins with her."

"Nor did she have any tools to cross to that castle."

No, she didn't have ropes or a grappling hook, but based on the note that had been left in his room the night of the fire, he was inclined to believe that the answer to his sister's disappearance lay somewhere in the castle. "There may be other ways to get across."

Noya eyed him as she handed him a plate of bacon and eggs. "You're not thinking of going back there, are you?"

"I..." He stammered. "I thought you weren't afraid. That you didn't believe the legends."

"I don't. But there's a darkness in those woods that attract evil, Liam. If we've lost Letty to it, I don't want to lose you too."

"All the more reason to search to see if we can find any sign of her or what happened to her, and to stop those that might have hurt her."

"You promised, Liam!"

"I know. I know. I will keep that promise. I swear it."

"Besides, you need to run the store."

"Yes, mother." He sighed and dug into his breakfast. But as he swallowed the runny eggs and chased it with another gulp of coffee, he couldn't help but think that the promise didn't say that he couldn't search the river South of the castle. And if there just so happened to be a way to cross over there, well he could always claim that he didn't know that it would lead him to those haunted hills.

Chapter Fifteen

The Lady's prayer asking for God to let her die and join her son was ignored.

At first, she thought it might have been granted. When she woke, her room was strangely quiet and cool. A fire burned in the fireplace, but it was barely more than ashes. The dim light it cast danced along the walls, bathing them in faint orange light. No, she thought, if she were dead, it would be significantly lighter. Filled with either the glory of angels, or the hellfire of demons. Or, if there was nothing beyond this life, it would be filled with nothing but darkness.

Her room was strangely quiet for once. There was no chanting, no whispered prayers or hushed conversations. All she could hear was the rattle of her breath in her chest. She looked around with bleary eyes, expecting someone to be sitting with her, but no priests or physicians or maids lurked in the shadows and the incense that irritated her so much was finally gone. Had they fallen victim to the plague as well? No, there were still people nearby; she could hear boots ringing on the stone courtyard outside her window and hear voices speaking on the other side of her door.

"We found her hiding in the old miller's house. She tried to make a run for it." A man said, and there was a thump as something was tossed or fell to the ground.

"Wouldn't you if you were being chased like rabbit by the hounds?" Someone new replied. This new voice was frail, that of an old woman.

"They say," Another man spoke, his voice deep and sonorous. "You have the gift. That you can know a way to stave off death."

"If I had that gift, would my family be dead and buried in a ditch?"

"I will give you anything you ask for."

"I told you I do not have any such ability."

"The carpenter says otherwise. He says his daughter owes her life to you."

"What I did for her is very different from what you ask me to do."

"Fine, if bribes will not work, then perhaps violence will. I know your son lives on. That he's been taken in by a family in Mill on Rye. If you do not do this, I will send my men and burn that place to the ground."

The old woman sighed. "Who would you have me try this miracle on?"

"The woman beyond that door. My wife."

"She is dying…"

"I can see that!" The second voice shouted. It was regal sounding, ringing through the carved wood and into her cold chamber. "I cannot risk taking it myself, and I cannot let any of my men test it for me. I need every one of them to keep the scum out."

"Like my husband and my children?"

A coughing fit wracked the Lady's body, but they ignored her, continuing their debate instead of coming to her aide.

"They were half dead. There was no saving them."

"The lady in there isn't much better off from the sounds of it. Why not let her go in peace? Enjoy the time you have left with her."

"She is the only one we can afford to lose!"

"But she's your..."

"I don't care! She deserves far worse for what she did!" The man snarled, his voice filled with hatred. "Give it to her. If she lives, we know that it works and you can make more for myself and my men. If she dies, then we know it doesn't, and you will shortly for join her for your lies."

Mattie found Rordan and Talesin waiting for her the next evening after Marionette's disastrous reveal. They were lounging outside of the door to her room, leaning against the dirty stone walls, inspecting nonexistent fingernails, and whistling as if they didn't have a care in the world. She glowered at them from the doorway, waiting for them to speak, to apologize for doubting her, but aside from Rordan's silly tune they remained silent.

After a few more notes of the twirling rise and fall of the little song, she finally gave in and spoke first. "Now do you believe me?"

"Oh, we never doubted you." Talesin replied.

"Not for a second." Rordan added.

"Excuse me! You claimed that I was just seeing things. That I imagined it."

"Actually, he was the one who said you imagined it. I said it was a doll." Rordan corrected her.

"No, I'm the one who said that it was probably just a doll." Talesin kicked at his brother's shins. "Which, technically, she kind of is. It looked like he had to do a bit of work to piece her together."

"Mmph." Mattie grunted. Realizing that this was probably the closest she would ever get to either of them admitting that she was right. "What do you think will happen to her?"

Talesin shrugged, his bony shoulders bobbing up and down underneath the thin fabric of his tunic. "The King has commanded that she will stay, so she'll learn to survive like the rest of us. Eat what you can when you can. Avoid the guards. So on and so forth."

"If she even lasts that long." His brother added. "She didn't look as if she were in very good shape, did she?"

"Well, it's not like she has anywhere to go. She can't go back home," Mattie noticed the brothers exchange a look at her words, but decided not to chase down that path at this time. "But she is fading fast. Wouldn't it be kinder for him to do what he did to the Chef?"

Talesin snorted. "Yes, because my head hanging from a pike is the way I'd like to spend the rest of my days, wouldn't you?"

"Maybe it's different for her, since she was made. Not cursed."

He shrugged, clearly not wanting to debate such a serious subject so early in the evening. "Perhaps. But the King has spoken, and what he says goes."

"Now. About the King..." Rordan drawled.

Mattie stiffened, instantly on guard. "What about him?"

"Since when have you become his little doll?"

"I am not his doll! I'm not anything to him!" She snapped. She could feel her cheeks flaming behind the mask she wore; the broken porcelain cool against her cheeks.

"Sure looked like something completely different last night, you perched at his feet like his pet."

"He saved me."

"From what?"

"His men. They found me in the library."

"Doing what?"

"Reading." It wasn't a total lie. She had been reading at first until Marionette showed up. The row of cages along the wall of the hidden room haunted her, what were they for? Had that been where the Toymaker kept his poor creation until her reveal or was there something more sinister behind the iron bars. "They didn't like my presence and were showing me how much they didn't like me in general when he showed up and stopped them. And then he invited me to the feast. And I couldn't say no after what he did for me."

Talesin snorted. "We've saved your skin plenty of times and you have no problem telling us no."

"That's different. He's the King."

"Right. Just because he has a crown..." His lips turned up in a snarl.

"Leave it." Rordan snarled right back at his brother.

Mattie sighed and rolled her eyes. "If this is the only reason why you came to see me, then I'm going back to bed."

The brothers exchanged another look that she couldn't quite read. After reaching some silent agreement, Rordan spoke. "It's not the only reason why we came."

"Oh?"

"How would you like to go on adventure?"

"What do you mean?"

"Get your darkest cloak and follow us."

"The last time I followed you, a grappling hook was involved and we almost got turned into dinner by the chef."

"C'mon - it'll be fun."

She snorted and turned to go back into her room. "I'm not sure I want any part of what you call fun."

"Wait," Talesin grabbed her hand, stopping her before she could slam the door in their faces. "I know we haven't given you much reason to like us lately, but trust me, this is something you'll want to see."

Mattie studied him from behind the safety of her mask. His expression was hard to read due to all the scarring on his face, but he seemed earnest enough. She sighed. "Fine. I'll go."

They moved quickly from shadow to shadow, halting many times for a guard or another citizen to pass. When they were unable to avoid the others, Talesin would lead her down a side corridor and they would lurk in a side room until they were sure they weren't being followed. Sometimes Rordan might make them double back just to be sure. But despite their best attempts at secrecy, there was no denying where they were leading her. The air around them became damper, and she could see moisture glimmering on the stone walls. Torches were few and far between.

Suddenly, far faster than Mattie expected it to, the heavy door to the dungeon loomed out of the darkness. She scowled at it as she studied the iron hinges and equally daunting locks. "What are we doing here?"

"You'll see." Talesin replied in a singsong tone. He tapped a rhythm out on the thick wood of the door and pressed his ear against it. After a moment, he pulled away. "He's not answering."

"Who's not answering?" Mattie asked, even though she knew she wouldn't get an answer from either of them.

"He never does." Rordan snapped. He tugged on the unwieldy iron ring. "C'mon and help me with this." Talesin sighed and joined him, and with many grunts and groans, they finally managed to open the door just wide enough for them to slip past.

Mattie eyed them as she stepped around them to peer into the darkness beyond the door. She didn't remember them having that much trouble the first time she had seen them entering the dungeon. Judging from their over exaggerated panting they were probably pretending that it was harder than it actually was in order to impress her. She reached out and pressed her hand against the rough wood planks of the door, yes it was heavy, but it moved easily under her touch. Someone had kept the hinges in working order despite the decay that threatened to take over the rest of the castle.

She glanced back at her companions and raised an eyebrow. They couldn't see it, but she guessed they could imagine what her expression looked like based on the embarrassed looks on their own faces. "What now?"

"You'll see." Rordan answered her.

"I'm getting awfully tired of being told that." She glanced down the steps leading down just beyond the opening of the door. "There's not some monster wanting to turn us into dinner like the chef is there?"

Talesin pulled a torch from a pile of supplies sitting just inside the opening. "Not a monster. Not exactly." He lit it with a flint he carried in his pocket. Much to Mattie's surprise, the rag wrapped around the top caught on the first strike. She thought that the damp air would have made it hard to light anything down here, but then the brothers had probably brought the bags and torches and stowed them away before coming to get her. "He can be a bit grouchy at times--"

Rordan snorted. "That's putting it mildly."

"-- But he's an okay fellow."

"Is he what you've brought me down here to see?" She took the torch from his hands.

He quickly went to work lighting another one which he passed off to his brother as soon as it was lit. "No. He's just the gatekeeper."

"The gatekeeper to what?"

"Well you're just full of questions tonight, aren't you?" Talesin's good humor snapped as the final torch caught flame.

"Wouldn't you have questions if you were in my place?" Mattie looked back at the stairs. "I've seen you come here before-"

Talesin was shocked. "You have?"

"You aren't the only one with secrets."

"Oh, if you only knew." He snorted at her reply. "What else have you seen?"

"I know you came back with food, because you were the only ones who were gone, and after you came back there was a feast in the Great Hall, so there must be storerooms down there."

He and his brother exchanged a look. "An astute observation."

"But it was fresh food, so I'm not sure how that's possible."

Another look passed between the two. Talesin opened his mouth to answer, but far off they could hear the clack of wooden heels against the stone floors. Rordan pushed them both forward into the doorway and down the first couple of steps. Mattie stumbled on the slick stone risers and put her hand out to steady herself. It came away covered with black slime and she wrinkled her nose in disgust, the motion lifting her mask away from her face enough for the cool air to wash across her skin.

"What was that for?!" Talesin snapped.

Rordan lifted his finger to his lips and pulled the door tightly behind them. Their torches flickered and danced in the draft. "Guards," He finally whispered and gestured for them to continue down the stairs.

Mattie sighed and took the steps downward carefully, one at a time. She slipped again about halfway down the staircase - in addition to being slippery, the steps were also uneven, and a few were cracked or had chunks missing. Thankfully Talesin was quick to catch her but her torch fell to the ground, tumbling down until it finally guttered out a few feet below her. She blew out a slow shaky breath. That had been far too close for her comfort.

"Careful." Rordan warned her. "This is the old part of the castle."

"Everything here is old." She replied.

"True. But this... this is even older than everything up above."

"That explains the state of the staircase, I guess."

"Now that," he gestured to the step she'd tripped over. It was shallower than all the others, and shorter as well - only a finger width or two above the one below it. "Is all deliberate. Not a result of age."

She could feel goosebumps prickling along her skin. She faintly remembered having this conversation with someone else, and for a moment, a vision of the King wavered in front of her. Malice tinted his normally friendly smile as if he was enjoying her discomfort, but that wasn't possible. She'd never been down here before. She gulped. "Why?"

"To prevent attacks." He slid past her, taking the lead since her torch had died. He held his own high overhead in an attempt to cast the light even farther around them.

"From what? Prisoners?"

"The outside."

"The outside?"

"You'll see." She groaned at his answer, and he chuckled as he led them deeper into the abyss.

Finally, they reached the bottom step. Mattie could see a large chamber stretching out before them, lined on either side with rusting bars. Cells, she realized after a moment, far larger and far more generous than the cages in her father's new workshop above.

The floor was covered in a thick layer of water that lapped at her shins when she stepped down into it. It seeped through the holes in her soles and around her feet, chilling her toes. If she thought the stairs were treacherous, she had to be especially careful here. One wrong step would see her flat on her rear end - something Rordan and Talesin would find endlessly entertaining. Far off she could hear the rolling boom of distant thunder. But it hadn't been stormy outside when she'd left her room, and the sound was continuous, echoing through the room.

"What is that?"

"The waterfall." Talesin held up his torch high overhead so she could see the full scope of the dungeons. However, the light did nothing to chase the darkness from the corners of the room. "We're right next to it."

"Oh." She pressed her hands against her ears to deafen the sound of the waterfall crashing against the rocks outside. She followed Rordan as he crossed the room, being careful to step as closely to where he did as possible. Water rippled away from them in tiny waves, splashing against the walls and heaven knew what else hiding in the shadows of the cells. "So where is all this food that you've been hoarding?" She asked, desperate to break the roaring silence.

"Nope. No food here." Talesin poked his torch into the cells, revealing that they held nothing but bones and other refuse.

"It would rot within a week." Rordan added. "This way. We're almost there."

"Are you sure that this is a wise idea?" A strange but oddly familiar voice asked from within one of the long-abandoned cells. A figure stepped forward out of the darkness he was lurking in, startling Mattie with his sudden appearance. He was dressed entirely in black, with a dark rag wrapped around the bottom half of his face. His cowl covered what the rag didn't, but his sharp blue eyes stood out despite the shadows. "If you go back there this quickly, it'll only raise suspicions."

"I'd rather deal with them out there than the idiots behind us." Talesin muttered. "Have you heard the latest news?"

Rordan scoffed. "Does he look like he's been outside this room since the last time we saw him?"

The shadow man ignored them. "What use have I for anything that happens above?"

"The king has left his tower, and the toymaker has made another." Talesin told him anyways.

Despite the man's claims that he didn't care, he stiffened at the news. "That's not possible. The Crone..."

"They found a way to do it without her."

"They're mad."

Mattie found herself stepping behind Rordan and Talesin as they spoke. Between the stranger's eyes and his voice, she felt as if the world around her was spinning. Tilting. It was if she had met him before, but for the life of her she couldn't remember when or where, and the fact that she couldn't remember left her aching in a way none of her other missed memories did. Those just left her feeling as if she were going mad. This made her feel as if she were overlooking something terribly important, and that her life would never be the same if she couldn't recall it.

Her movement, small though it was, attracted the man's attention. She shivered as his unnatural gaze settled on her. "Who is this?"

"No one." Rordan answered at the same time Talesin said, "A comrade in arms."

"She's small." Was the stranger's reply. "She doesn't look like she'll be able to carry much. Are you sure she's worth it?"

"Always."

"She's stronger than she looks." Talesin dropped his arm over Mattie's shoulders. She stumbled under the sudden weight.

"Hmf." Was all the man had to say about that. He stepped out of the cell and led them deeper into the dungeon, moving effortlessly through the darkness without any light. He stopped before a rack of weapons hanging on the far wall. The metal blades of the axes and flails were rusty, and the wooden poles were black with mold, but a sword nearby glinted in the torchlight. It appeared that the stranger spent all his time caring for it and it alone. There were other instruments hanging on the wall - smaller knives and hooks covered in gummy grime that had nothing to do with the conditions around them. Mattie looked away rather than study them for too long.

The man felt along the edge of the rack, his long pale fingers searching for something. He stopped and pressed in on what appeared to be a crack in the wood, and a click echoed through the dungeon. The rack slid to one side to reveal another imposing door crisscrossed with iron strips.

Even though this door appeared to be in just as good shape as the door at the top of the stairs, it was far, far heavier. It took both Talesin, Rordan, and the strange man to pull it open while Mattie stood back and held the torches. Once it was ajar, she soon spotted the reason why - the opposite side of the door was covered in a thick layer of iron and metal spikes.

The roar of the waterfall was almost deafening now, and fresh water poured through the entryway and pooled around their feet. If Mattie thought the water in the dungeon was already cold, this wave turned her legs into ice. Her feet felt like lead, heavy and cumbersome, as Rordan and Talesin ushered her through to the other side.

The stranger shut the door behind them as soon as they passed the threshold, and she could hear the grinding of metal against stone as the locks slid into place. She cried out, "He's locking us in!"

"No." Talesin corrected her as he stepped past her. He had to shout to be heard over the roar echoing around them. "He's locking us out. Look!" He held up his torch so she could see where they stood, and her mouth fell open.

In front of them a wall of water thundered over the cliffs overhead to crash against the rocks below their feet. Mattie stuck her hand out, her fingers cutting through the cascade to scatter droplets through the air.

The waterfall.

They were behind the waterfall.

And beyond the waterfall, she could see the open night sky, trees that were vibrant in the moonlight, and fresh cool air that didn't smell of rot, or dust, or death.

They were outside the castle.

Chapter Sixteen

Talesin and Rordan led Mattie down a narrow path that was cut into the cliff side. The trail was slippery from the fine mist that endlessly pelted it and she kept one hand on the roughly hewn solid rock to steady herself as she crept along. At least it was clean of muck and mire. Every now and then she glanced behind her, watching as more and more of the castle was revealed through the currents of the waterfall.

They were truly outside.

They were going to see trees. Flowers. Animals. People.

She wanted to sing and dance in joy. But, since the pathway was so treacherous, she kept her excitement under control as they inched along. She could celebrate once they were on more solid ground.

Ahead of her, Rordan and Talesin walked with their heads down, their torches held between their bodies and the rocks to shield them from the spray of the water. They were not as awed as she was by the sight of the castle looming behind them. Why would they be? They had made this trip several times over the years, carrying food from the village to the castle whenever they felt the villagers had enough to spare. It suddenly occurred to her that they were probably the ones she'd seen the night she dropped her mask.

"When was the last time you came out here?" Mattie called out to them, shouting to be heard over the crash of the waterfall.

"Have you forgotten already? The night of the great feast, of course." Rordan shouted back. "The night you told us that you didn't trust us!"

"We also left that message, remember?" Talesin giggled. His brother reached back and slapped at him, but he easily dodged the attack by scooting backwards.

"I mean, what about before?" Mattie asked again, stepping back herself lest she be caught up in their battle.

"Oh... I'm not sure. Maybe three months ago... or it could be four. Why?"

"Hm." It hadn't been that long ago that she had found Marionette in her father's workshop. If it wasn't them behind the waterfall that night, who could it have been? The man from the dungeon didn't seem inclined to go out exploring. "Does anyone else know about this?"

Talesin shook his head. "No."

"I'm sure a few do." Rordan corrected him. "But our friend back there only lets us through. He boards up the door for everyone else and pretends he's not home."

"Ah." Mattie let her hand fall away from the wall as the path twisted away from the waterfall and into a cave. The torches danced in the gusts of air that brushed past them, and a tiny stream, barely more than a trickle, flowed past their feet. The tunnel grew smaller, until the ceiling of it brushed against their hair and they were forced to bend over to continue.

She was starting to think that she would never see the sky again when the tunnel finally opened up once more, dumping them out onto a hillside that was covered with brush and trees. She inhaled deeply, breathing in the crisp fresh scent of pine and late fall wildflowers. She giggled, then laughed, and then ran down the hill with her arms wide open.

When Rordan and Talesin finally caught up with Mattie, they explained where they were and what the plan was while they trekked through the woods.

"There's a village not too far away that didn't succumb to the plague when it came through. Nor did its members decide to abandon it." Rordan explained.

"Mmhm." Mattie hummed, trying to focus but still amazed at their surroundings. She could hear owls hooting in the distance, and saw the glow of green eyes as a fox studied them for a moment before darting off into a bush.

"When things get a little tight, we come out and take a little extra to help us along."

"Why?" She asked. Food, even real food like she had tasted the night before, did nothing to stop the hunger in their bellies.

Talesin turned towards her. "Would you rather things dissolve into chaos again? Consider yourself lucky that you don't remember the dark times."

"Things drastically improved once we started bringing supplies in." Rordan continued.

"We never take more than we need -"

"- So we don't arouse suspicions."

"Exactly." Rordan paused for a moment while Talesin stepped past him to scout ahead. The trees were starting to thin out, and the danger of being seen grew higher and higher as a result. "The last thing we needed was more of us trying to sneak out here, or them down there coming and trying to break down our doors."

They crept forward after Talesin gave them to signal that it was all clear. Off in the distance Mattie could make out the silhouettes of houses, their windows glowing with light. Around the town were fields with crops planted in neat rows and she could hear cows lowing in their pens.

"Do they have horses?" She asked suddenly, thinking of the gilded pictures she'd seen in the library.

"And dogs, and cats, and sheep. Even mice and rats." Talesin chuckled from his spot behind a tree.

"I wouldn't try calling any of them over to you though. They won't come near us." Rordan chimed in.

"Why?" Mattie asked.

Both brothers stopped and looked at her, and she immediately felt like an idiot. "Look at us. What living thing would want anything to do with us?"

"Right." She had been so caught up in the thrill of being outside that she'd temporarily forgotten about the curse. Just like all living things avoided the castle, except for the occasional idiotic villager, anything out here would try to avoid them as well. "What about the villagers?"

"Most are in bed, except for a few drunken idiots." Rordan stomped in a mud puddle, thick globs of dirty water splashing everyone.

Talesin threw a rock at him. "They're easy enough to get around - if you want to."

"What do you mean, if you want to?" She stepped back, out of the range of the two brothers now tossing sticks and other things back and forth.

"Sometimes we have a little fun with them."

"They're very superstitious folk, our neighbors."

Mattie glanced between them, her jaw hanging open in surprise. "But the King said we're not to be seen!"

Rordan danced around her, leaning close to whisper in her ear. "I don't know if you've noticed, but the King isn't exactly here right now."

"But -"

"We're not actually being seen..." Talesin started.

"... it's more like a brief glimpse." Rordan continued. "We're in and out before they've even realized what's happened."

"It doesn't hurt them; we just jump out and yell boo and they get scared." Talesin smiled. "We don't even touch them."

"It's just teasing them. It's all in good fun. They even laugh about it afterwards." Rordan swatted at a bush with a stick.

Mattie rolled her eyes; she didn't understand how getting scared could be considered fun.

"It'll take your mind off of things." One of the brothers suggested.

"There's nothing like jumping out from the shadows in front of a villager and watching them run off screaming to lift the spirits." The other one shoved him out of the way.

"Fine." Mattie sighed. "Let's go."

"In time, in time." Rordan promised her. "First, we get some food. Can't scare anyone on an empty stomach after all."

That was how Mattie found herself crouching behind some bushes an hour or so later.

Rucksacks full of stolen goods sat around her feet as she eyed the building the brothers called a pub. It was squat and ugly thing located on the very edge of the village. Made of roughly hewn boards with no windows, the ground around it stunk of piss, vomit, and something yeasty. However, despite the smell, the men of the village seemed to be called to it; a steady stream of male villagers had been coming and going ever since her friends had led her to the bushes a short distance away.

"They should be leaving soon," Rordan whispered in her ear. "They always leave around this time."

Mattie looked up at the moon in the sky. It was getting rather late; sneaking into barns and root cellars and digging through food to find the worst pieces that wouldn't be missed had taken far longer than she thought it would. However, the raucous singing from within the pub didn't seem like it would be dying down anytime soon. She glanced at her friends – if something didn't happen soon, they should probably get started back to the tunnels if they wanted to make it inside the safety of the castle before sunrise.

The door to the pub swung open suddenly, and the noise increased as a man stumbled out into the street. He wove back and forth as he wandered towards where they hid. Talesin tapped Mattie on the shoulder and pointed at the Survivor. "Him! Go after him!"

Eager to get this over and done with, she did what her friends told her to and jumped out of the shadows in front of the man with a cry and waved her hands above her head menacingly. The man yelped, his eyes rolled back into his head and he collapsed in a heap on the ground. She stared down at him in surprise – was he dead?

Rordan and Talesin quickly pulled her back into the shadows as more men poured out of the pub, summoned by the noise their fellow villager made while collapsing. They listened as he raved about the life-sized doll he'd seen and pointed in the direction that Mattie had ran away in, but instead of looking for her, his friends just pulled him to his feet and dragged him back into the pub.

Rordan and Talesin dissolved into fits of laughter while Mattie gaped after the man and his comrades.

"Want to try another one?" Rordan asked when he could breathe again.

"Sure." It was a powerful feeling to realize that a little thing like her could make a grown man faint. She ran her fingers over the cracks it as she followed brothers to another pub that she knew of.

"We won't be able to scare anyone there again for a couple of days." Talesin explained. "Once or twice every couple of months or so is safe. Anything more than that and it puts them on guard."

He darted across a garden behind a house, but Rordan grabbed the back of Mattie's shirt before she could follow. When she turned to scold him for startling her so he held a finger against his lips, "Watch and learn."

A little girl opened the door in the back of the house. She peered into the darkness, a determined look on her sweet face, before jumping down the steps that lead to the garden and bolting along a little path that ended at a small building at the very back of the yard.

Mattie felt her blood run cold at the sight of the child. She knew what Talesin was going to do – he was going to scare her like she had scared the drunkard -

and suddenly she felt like the monster the drunkard thought she was. She wanted to stop it, to cry out and warn the girl, but Rordan was strong, and he held her back easily.

The girl was almost to the door of the building when Talesin stepped out in front of her. "Where are you going?" He lowered his voice to a growl. "I thought I told you not to come back here!"

The girl shrieked at the sight of his mangled visage and ran back towards the house, a dark stain spreading across the skirt of her nightgown as she went.

"Good one!" Rordan clapped his brother on the shoulder when they reached him, a grin spreading across his twisted face – well, as much as he could grin.

"Thank you! That one is always fun to mess with!" Talesin bowed then turned to Mattie, "See? Didn't we tell you this would take your mind off things?"

She smacked the back of his head. "Idiot!"

"What? What did I do now?!"

"She's just a child!"

"Her parents probably fill her head with stories every night about us and the castle! Villagers always do!" He defended himself. "Even if I hadn't been here she probably would have been scared by something else! An owl, a rat, a bush! Anything!"

Mattie opened her mouth to continue to scold him, but the back door to the house banged open, filling the yard with bright light. The three Undying Ones turned to find that the child had summoned her mother to her defense. The woman stared at them, her jaw hanging open for a moment or two in surprise, and then she screamed. The windows of the houses nearby began to open and other villagers popped their heads out of them, looking for the source of the commotion.

"Run!" Rordan cried. They dropped the bags of stolen food they were carrying and bolted through the garden. They ran by another house that opened its door just as they passed. Mattie caught a glimpse of an old man staring at them in puzzlement as someone - the father of the girl she assumed - fired his crossbow into the air above their heads and shouted after them. The bolt landed with a thud in the ground just in front of them and she nearly tripped over it in her desperation to avoid the villagers.

They zigged and zagged, deeper and deeper into the village. Finally, when they felt that they were safe enough, they stopped behind a shed to catch their breath. From inside of it, Mattie could hear a cow lowing and smell the pungent aroma of fresh manure. But even something so foul couldn't compare to the decay of the castle.

Rordan laughed in between gasps of air. "Well, that was fun. How about we go find that other pub now?"

Mattie looked back the way they had come, "You can go find it, I'm going to go get our food."

"Why bother – we can hit up some other houses on the way back to the castle."

"They're probably all locked tight by now!" She hissed, keeping her voice low in case there was something besides a cow in the shed at their backs. "Who knows if we'll be able to get anything else after tonight."

"Word doesn't spread that quickly unless there's a fire. I promise you, the other cellars will still be open and ripe for the picking." Talesin draped an arm around her shoulders."

"At the very least shouldn't we go back and hide the evidence?"

"Why bother? They'll just assume it's some gypsy. They always do. And sure, they may lock their doors and sleep a little lighter, but in a fortnight they'll forget again and it'll be back to business as usual."

"You worry too much, pet."

"I'd rather worry too much than be too careless and be the reason why a mob shows up at our door." She stepped out from under his arm and started back towards the house with the girl and the garden. She knew she wouldn't be able to grab the bags just yet; the family and their neighbors would still be awake and excited by the chaos they had created. She would have to find herself a shed or a bush to hide in and wait until they settled down before she made her move.

"Oh, come on! You'll be missing out!"

"Let her go. We'll meet you at where the tunnel leaves the hill." Rordan pulled his brother away. He lowered his voice to a whisper so she wouldn't hear what he said next. "You know how she gets when she's set on something, besides this is the perfect opportunity."

Mattie froze – what did he mean how she got when she was set on something? She always did what they suggested! And perfect opportunity for what? She turned to face them, but they were already gone.

Chapter Seventeen

Two houses down from the house with the garden was a building that had a lean-too on the back of it. It was currently being used to store firewood, but there was enough space between the cords of wood that Mattie could slip inside.

She crawled in just in time; just after she'd settled herself amongst the split logs a villager man walked past carrying a lantern and a short sword. An idea occurred to her as she watched his shadow blend into the night: maybe, if he was slow to make his rounds, she could run out and grab the bags before he made it back. She counted quietly, waiting to see how long it would take for him to appear again - it took the man almost three counts to one hundred to pass by again. Yes, she thought to herself, she could make it as long as she left immediately after he passed her hiding spot.

Mattie inched her way closer to the entrance of the lean-too and tucked her legs underneath her so she would be ready the next time the man came around. She waited for the man to pass, and as soon as he was out of sight she jumped out and ran towards the garden where Talesin had scared the little girl. The bags were exactly where she dropped them in the bushes that separated this yard from the next. As she scooped them up, she could hear the villager whistling to himself as he drew near. She ducked down, underneath the bushes, and pulled her cloak tightly around her. When she was sure the garden was safe once again, she rose out of the shadows.

The little girl was standing on the path. Behind her, her mother stood in the doorway of the house. Thankfully the older woman was turned away from the garden, probably speaking with someone within Mattie assumed, and was not paying attention to what was going on behind her.

Mattie pressed a finger against the lips on her mask. The girl watched her with wide eyes as she crossed the garden to the other side, and passed through the bushes that marked the boundary between it and the next house. She thought that she just might make her escape without any problems, when suddenly the girl began to scream for her mother. Mattie couldn't help but flinch at the terror in her voice - terror that she had caused – even if it was unintentional. She longed to turn back, to reassure the girl that she was not a monster, but she bolted instead. Any villagers patrolling the area might catch her with the stolen food if she lingered too long.

She neared a street, but didn't stop to check to make sure that it was clear before she crossed it. Instead she continued to run at full speed, desperate to put as much distance between her and the house with the garden as possible. She collided with something hard and fell to the ground in a tangle of limbs and smashed fruit and bread.

The thing under her groaned in pain. Mattie opened her eyes and found herself staring into the face of a young man with bright red hair – red like Marionette. Red like the villager she'd seen standing on the bridge.

The man groaned again and opened his eyes, "Letty?"

Mattie tried to jump away, but the villager grabbed her wrist, holding her against him. "Let me go!"

"No! D'ya know how long you've been gone? Ma's worried sick about ya." His words slurred together and his breath reeked of ale and other spirits. He stood, jerked her to her feet, and started to tug her along the road.

"You're drunk and confused!"

"I've never been more sober in my life. C'mon. Ma will be so excited."

"I'm not Letty!" Mattie continued to fight him; scratching at his arm and trying to kick him – anything to break his grip.

He shook her in response, and she felt her head snap back and forth on her neck. She was suddenly grateful for the curse; such a move would have killed any other girl. "Why are you fighting me? Don't you want to go home? And why are you wearing that silly mask?" He reached forward to pull her mask off her face but she leaned backwards and his fingers closed on empty air. He frowned at her and some sort of clarity seemed to finally dawn in his grey eyes. "Wait, you're not Letty…"

"That's what I've been trying to tell you, you oaf!"

In the distance, they could hear the baying of hounds. The man looked in the direction the noise was coming from. "What's all that racket about? Who are you? What have you been up to?"

Mattie took advantage of the distraction to kick him. This time she did it where it mattered; in his groin, like Rordan and Talesin had shown her so many years ago. The villager cried out in pain and doubled over. She swung the bag and hit him on the head with it and he dropped to the ground. Finally free, Mattie turned and ran for the forest.

She didn't stop running until she reached the tunnel.

Neither Talesin nor Rordan were waiting for her like they said they would be.

There were signs that they had been there. Their torches were gone, and muddy footprints led into the depths of the small cave that marked the entrance to the tunnel. She crawled in after them, thinking that she might be able to catch up, but they were already gone - the door on the other side of the waterfall closed fast.

She stood there before it, looking up at the heavy wood and iron bindings. The row upon row of spikes meant to keep invaders out. Perhaps she was wrong. Perhaps she hadn't missed them. Perhaps she'd beaten them back and they were waiting for her at the entrance to the tunnel. She crept back the way she'd come, making sure to step carefully so she wouldn't slip and smash herself against the rocks below. Being trapped there in the rushing water for the rest of eternity did not seem like a desirable way to spend one's time.

When Mattie reached the entrance again, Rordan and Talesin were still missing. There was nothing except for the grass and trees, and the occasional brave fox peering at her from behind a tree. She licked her lips as she stared at the lights of the village off in the distance. Maybe they were still gathering food then. They were cutting it awfully close if they were, the moon would be setting soon, and the sun would start to rise shortly after that. But they were more familiar with the outside world than she was, so she could only assume that they knew what they were doing.

She lingered by the entrance, sometimes walking down to the edge of the trees, sometimes sitting just inside the cave. To pass the time, she threw small stones at the rock walls, or sent them skittering down the hill. She munched on an old withered apple and then a bit of old moldy cheese. Meanwhile the moon sank lower and lower, and there was still no sign of Talesin or Rordan.

She began to believe that her first assumption was right. They arrived here before her, and rather than wait for her, they'd abandoned her. But why? What had she done to make them turn on her so? Sure, she disagreed with their idea of fun, but they'd had disagreements before, and while they might go through periods of avoiding each other as a result, they didn't exactly turn their backs on one another. Especially if they needed help. So, what did she do to deserve this?

If the brothers, her best friends, wouldn't help her, then maybe the guardian of the dungeon would. As much as she disliked the disorienting effect he had on her, it was better than sitting out here, waiting for the sun to burn her into ashes.

At the edge of the horizon, the sky above the trees started to turn a lighter shade of black. As Mattie watched, it continued to grow into a deep shade of purple. Hissing to herself, she quickly crept back inside the cave. She followed the tunnel back to the waterfall, and then rushed over the narrow path to the iron door. Her feet slipped and slid on the slick rock, but she managed to reach the other side in one piece.

She banged on the door, making sure to avoid the iron spikes. "Hey! Hey! Let me in! The sun is coming!"

The door remained shut. She pressed an ear against it, but she could hear nothing over the sound of the waterfall pouring around her. Perhaps he couldn't hear her either. She slammed her fists on the old iron once more, as hard as she could. She would be bruised in the morning, but it was better than the alternative.

Still the door remained shut.

She continued to bang and scream, until her muscles ached and her voice was gone, all the while praying that the man she knew on the other side would hear her and let her in. When the powers that be deemed not to answer that prayer, she prayed that Rordan and Talesin would take pity on her instead. Or that they would finally open it and tell her it was all just a joke and she was getting worked up over nothing.

But still the door remained shut.

The sky was a faded shade of grey now - almost white - and the sun was just starting to peek over the horizon. It was a brilliant sliver of light that made her eyes water. For a moment, she considered just sitting down and letting the sun take her with its powerful rays. Then the next time the brothers went scavenging, they would find her ashes waiting for them and maybe they might feel some remorse for what had happened.

Instead she crawled back along the pathway, making it to the safety of the tunnel just as the sun cleared the horizon. She inched further and further down into the safety of darkness until she found a spot where she could huddle that wasn't damp nor threatened by bright day light. She wrapped her cloak around her as she curled up on the hard stone floor.

"My name is Mattie, I am the only child of the Toymaker and his wife. His wife died long before the bad times when I was a babe." She murmured to herself, falling into the old familiar comfort of the words she whispered to herself every night. "My father was a favorite of the Queen. She is the one who convinced the King to take pity on us when the plague came. The castle was cursed by a..." She stumbled over her nightly litany, wondering what exactly caused the citizens of the castle to become what they were – but she was too tired to pursue the thoughts any further. "Whatever cursed us, it is why we are still alive today when so many others died.

"My father has turned a villager into a doll. I don't know how he got her body, but he did. My friends insisted it was only my imagination... and I... I was afraid that they were right." She admitted to darkness. "But my father presented the doll to the King last night, and now everyone knows I'm not crazy.

"Rordan and Talesin took me out of the castle today. I stole food from their barns and pantries. I was seen by Villagers, and I scared them. Rordan and Talesin said it was safe. But one man grabbed me because he thought I was someone else." Though how he had confused her with a village girl was beyond her. They wore pretty frocks and did their hair up in curls and bows while she wore rags and her hair hadn't been touched by a comb since before the bad times. Her breath hitched as she spoke her next words. "Rordan and Talesin abandoned me. I've been locked out of the castle, and I don't know how to get back in."

"I am a hundred, two months and...." She opened her eyes, trying to remember the most recent marks in her bedroom. "Fourteen days old."

The next time the lady woke the room was darker; the candles had burned down until they were only as tall as the width of her finger, and the fire in her fireplace was no longer roaring. An old woman sat in front of it, staring absently into the flames.

"Water. I need water." She begged. The woman was not one of her normal maids but she was so thirsty. This fever was burning her alive, but the doctors refused to let her drink anything but their noxious medicines and tinctures for the past three days as they bled her and drained the bulbos that marked her body. "Please."

"I don't have water for you, dearie." The old woman said and turned to face her. She looked like a witch from the old stories with skin was paper thin and wrinkled, and hair that was whiter than snow. "I do have some tea I brewed just for you."

"No." The lady shook her head. "No more potions."

The old woman made a tutting noise, "Now, dearie, don't be a child – this will make you better."

"They all say that." She laughed, but only a wispy sound escaped her lips. "But they can't. I am dying. We all will. This sickness will kill us all. Nothing can stop it."

"This will."

"No, it won't." The lady insisted. She stared at the woman, remembering the voices she had heard earlier. "It was you, wasn't it? You were speaking with him about me..." Another cough wracked her body.

The old woman's bones creaked and cracked as she stood and approached the bed. "Those were just waking dreams, dearie. They're sometimes brought on by fevers like yours."

"Leave me." Her command sounded weak rather than ringing with the authority and power she used to hold.

"Come now. Just a sip and it will all be over." The old woman was surprisingly strong. Even though the lady turned her head to prevent the old woman from touching her, the crone grabbed the back of her head and forced her to face forward and then tipped the tankard against her lips. The lady kept her mouth shut, and the noxious tea spilled onto the bed instead, but then the fumes filled her nose. She started to cough. The liquid filled her mouth in between gasps for air and she was forced to swallow the foul-tasting liquid prevent from choking. Once the tankard was empty, the old woman finally released her and patted her hand absently. *"See? Now was that so bad?"*

"When my…" She started to say, but the rest of her words died on her lips. No, he wouldn't do anything if he heard about this; after all, he had been the one who sent the old woman to her chambers. She supposed she deserved it for betraying him like she did, but she couldn't help but cry in frustration. To go from being blessed with good health and beauty to being sick and frail, to have a legion of men and servants you could command to having nothing… She turned away so the old woman would not see her tears.

Chapter Eighteen

When the moon rose once again, Mattie crept out of her hiding spot in the tunnel. She had no desire to return to the village after the previous night. No doubt that the villagers would be protecting their pantries and children against any unwanted visitors and she didn't want any part of the chaos that might ensue if someone caught her wandering around.

She returned to the entrance of the tunnel to find that her bag full of food had been disturbed during the day. Some brave creature stole the cheese and dried meat from canvas rucksack, but left her the apples. She munched on one, savoring the dribble of juice that trickled down her throat. It was very rare that she ever ate more than one meal a day - even with all the contributions that Rordan and Talesin made to the kitchen - so the small apple was a luxury. Once it was finished, she tossed the core to the side and dragged the bag back into the tunnel with her. She found a crack in the tunnel wall to store it that was safe from dampness and easy for her to reach but hopefully far enough off the ground that it wouldn't be bothered by animals.

Then she made the short trek back to the door.

It was still closed tight, and no matter how loud she screamed or pounded on the door, nothing happened. It remained firmly shut. Still, she sat by it that night, and the next, and the next, waiting and waiting for Rordan and Talesin to return.

They never did.

On the fifth night, Mattie gave up. It was clear that either no one could hear her, or they could but they didn't. And it might be months before Rordan and Talesin came out to go scavenging again. For all she knew, they could have barrels of food tucked away somewhere in the bowels of the castle. She was on her own.

Her little stash of apples was running low, and she'd picked all the berries she could find near the cave. She didn't know how to hunt or set traps, and even if she did, the animals who lived nearby abandoned the area shortly after her arrival. It was time for her to start exploring the world beyond the forest, and do a little scavenging on her own.

The next day she rose before the sun disappeared from the sky, and grabbed her last apple from her stash. She hiked down the hill and through the trees, kicking at rocks and leaves, and trying to mimic the calls of the wild life around her. However, that only resulted in a couple of close calls with hunters – not even the forest was as safe as she thought it was.

She considered racing back up the hill to the safety of the cave. She could survive without food. She had done it often enough during the bad years, after the curse first took hold. But after indulging in regular meals the past few days, even if it was only apples and berries, she didn't fancy the idea of going back to eating nothing.

Off in the distance the lights of the village glowed like stars against the dark shadows of the forest. They taunted her with the promise of fresh food. More apples, and berries. Bread and fresh cheese. Carrots and onions. Maybe even a bit of meat.

It had been awhile since the incident with the drunkards and the child. Surely they had forgotten about their encounter with her by now. If she waited until well after the pubs closed before wandering the streets and lanes she should be safe. By then even the bully boys would be tucked into their beds with charms hanging over their doors to ward off evil, and the one or two brave souls who still patrolled the streets would be sleepy and sluggish. If she was careful and didn't set off any alarms, she should be able to walk around without being discovered.

So Mattie waited, biding her time, and when the moon was at its apex, she slipped through the trees and past the farms. She did pause here and there to pluck this fruit from the vine, or weasel this vegetable out of the ground on the way. She stopped at a root cellar that Rordan had showed her, and filled her sack with cheese and potatoes. After a moment, she took a couple of jars of preserves off the shelf - making sure to grab the dustier ones in the back - and added them to her bag. They should taste good on bread, but sadly, the farm wife hadn't left any loaves sitting out.

Maybe she might find something in the village...

A glance at the sky outside the cellar told her that the moon was starting to set. Dawn wasn't far off, and if she wanted to make it back to the safety of the caves before the sun's bright light washed over the valley, she would need to hustle. Sighing, she started the long hike back to the cave. Even if she hadn't gotten everything she wanted, she had more than enough to last her for a few days.

When the sun set the next day though, she felt restless. Yes, there was enough food for the moment, but the thought of sitting around all day, doing nothing but twiddling her thumbs, irked her. Sure, she had hidden in her room often enough at the castle. But she was no longer in the castle. She was free to go where ever she wanted, whenever she wanted, without any fear of the guards harming her. She still needed to be careful of the villagers, but even though they outnumbered her, they paled in comparison to what she saw day in and day out, year after year after year inside the castle walls.

Mattie set out earlier the following night. As soon as she ate her breakfast meal, she stepped out of the cave and started the long hike down the hill to the village. She made sure to skirt around the farm she stole from the night before - just in case they had noticed anything missing - and once she passed it, she lingered at the edge of the village, waiting for the drunkards to abandon the pub before she moved any further. Once the last soul abandoned the streets, she stepped out of the shadows and surveyed her domain.

Before, when Mattie visited the village with Rordan and Talesin she had only been looking for food. She hadn't bothered to look at what was inside the barns and sheds beyond the supplies that sat on the shelves. She didn't want to startle any of the animals that might be sleeping there, so she'd run in, grabbed what she needed, and ran back out. Now she paused to gander at the creatures that called these rough buildings home. For the most part, the cows ignored her. They stood, chewing their cud - pausing only to drink water out of the basins sitting in the corner. The horses, however, seemed a little more interested in her existence. The great beasts sniffed at her hand and lipped at her fingers, looking for apples and carrots while regarding her quietly with solemn dark eyes. Despite their size, they were gentle creatures, and their skin was velvety soft. And to her complete and utter surprise, they weren't afraid of her like the wildlife around the cave was.

Mattie was attracted to one horse in particular that she found in a barn outside of the largest house in the village. Where the other horses were sturdy workers, built for pulling wagons and ploughs, this creature was small and dainty and its eyes were bright with intelligence. Much like the others, it was fond apples, and so Mattie would perch on the railing of its stall and fed it bits of apple she'd stolen from a lean to earlier in the night, smiling to herself when it would demand more by pulling at her clothes with its teeth.

She visited it again the next night, and the night after that, and soon she considered the beast her new best friend. Unlike Rordan and Talesin, the horse didn't have any secrets. And it didn't judge or abandon her. It was waiting patiently for her at the front of the stall every evening, it's ears flicked forward as it listened for her approach. All it wanted from her was an apple and a good shoulder rub, and it was happy.

Perhaps, she thought, as she perched on the edge of the stall on yet a different night, this being trapped outside of the castle thing wasn't so bad after all. She didn't need to worry about the King staring at her, the guards hunting her, or Rordan and Talesin's twisted games. She did miss her father, but if she were truly honest with herself, she had lost him to his madness ages ago. And while strange dreams still bothered her from time to time, at least she didn't feel haunted at every turn.

Here, she could just be herself.

Chapter Nineteen

    The family store was deader than the pubs on a holy day. Liam leaned his shoulder against the thick glass windows, watching as the people of Mill-on-Rye strolled by. Some crossed the street rather than be tainted by the Mercat's shame. Others looked away as they passed, and whispered to their fellows in hushed tones. Eventually they would need salt, or sugar, or even fabric for clothing. They would sneak in right before sundown, or maybe at first light, and they would smile and pretend as if nothing had ever happened, but they would be glancing over their shoulders the whole entire time to make sure that their friends weren't watching. Then they would slip back out and go straight back to ignoring Mercat's until they needed something again.

    Liam sighed. He longed to yell at them, to point them to the sections of the holy book that spoke against hypocrisy. But he knew it was pointless. Nothing would change his fellow villager's attitude - they would continue to shun them until another family slipped up.

And then all would be forgotten until something reminded them of the Mercat's shame.

He finally turned away from the windows and strolled around the store, looking for something to keep him busy. He'd already swept the floors twice today, and dusted until the shelves were clean enough that the local clergy would eat off them. All the fabrics his father had ordered earlier in the summer were arranged so that they resembled a rainbow, and the leather books were in alphabetical order - thanks to his mother's help. He supposed he could go over the numbers one last time, but he didn't fancy giving himself a headache this early in the day.

A glance at the spices shelved behind the counter revealed that they were a little disorderly, and the candy was running a little low. He hopped over the thick wooden countertop and set about spacing the spices so the jars were lined up like soldiers waiting for battle. And they had quite a battle ahead of them, he thought with a snort. He'd noticed over the years that the women who bought the most spices were some of the worst cooks in Mill-on-Rye. Apparently, they seemed to think that quantity was equal to quality.

The bells attached to the door jingled, and Liam looked up from the jars he was straightening to see one of Mill-on-Rye's many hunters standing at the counter. "Hello, Jack. What do you have for me today? Some venison? A bear pelt?"

"Nothing so nice, Liam. Nothing so nice." Jack leaned against the counter. He drummed his fingers on the dark grain of the wood, and he seemed to find everything in the store infinitely more interesting than the man running it, even though he'd been in here hundreds of times before. Finally, he sucked in a deep breath and met Liam's eyes. "There's no way to put this easily - I found something just South of the castle."

"Found what?" Liam asked. He leaned against the shelves behind him and studied the hunter standing before him, waiting expectantly for the man to explain his presence. Jack normally only came into the store when he had something to trade, and he was usually very direct and friendly. To see him acting like a tongue-tied buffoon filled Liam's stomach with gnawing swirling dread.

The hunter fidgeted under his gaze, shifting his balance from foot to foot and slipping his hands into his pockets only to pull them back out a moment later. Finally, he extracted a plaid handkerchief that was knotted multiple times around something small and dainty as if it might fly away if it wasn't properly tethered in place. He undid the knots, revealing something silver that shined in the dim light of the lanterns hanging around the store.

Liam froze when his mind finally processed what the hunter was holding - a locket on a delicate strand of pearls. It was almost identical to the one that his sister always wore, but it was hard to tell from so far away. He held out his hand, and Jack dropped the necklace onto his palm. The minute it hit his hand he knew. He didn't want to believe it, but he knew. Maybe, he thought as he turned it over, it wasn't hers. Maybe, it belonged to another girl from the village. But he knew that was wrong - only one girl in Mill-on-Rye ever dared to wear something so fancy. Only one girl came from a family that made enough money to purchase something so fine.

Taking a deep breath to steady himself, he popped it open. There was the engraved message from his grandfather on the inside of the locket, and the strand of his grandmother's hair on the other side. He swore. "You found this South of the castle you said?"

Jack nodded.

"Was there anything else?"

"Dried blood, lots of it, on the rocks next to the rapids."

"But no sign of a body?"

"No." For a moment, hope flared in Liam's heart, but the hunter's next words were grim. "But no one can lose that much and still live."

"I wouldn't be so sure about that. Letty is a smart girl. She's strong."

"She's also been out there for over a month. A month. With no food or water." Jack finally caught his eye. His expression was earnest, willing him to understand, but Liam refused to accept it.

"Don't say that."

"If she somehow was able to survive, then why hasn't she returned?"

"You know why she wouldn't. Everyone in town knows why."

"Winter is drawing closer every day, my friend, and then there are the creatures to consider. She may be the bravest and smartest girl around - but those things aren't exactly human."

"Stop talking!" Liam snarled. A part of him knew that Jack was right, but his heart still refused to give up hope. "You know those creatures are nothing but old wives' tales. There's nothing out there. Nothing!"

The hunter snorted. "Tell that to the baker's daughter." He reached out and grabbed Liam's forearm. "I'm sorry, friend. I am so very sorry. None of us wanted it to end this way."

"Enough!" Liam jerked his arm away. The locket flew out of his hand in the process and went flying across the room. It crashed against the wall - right next to the doorway his mother was currently walking through.

Jack sketched a quick bow in her general direction. "Ma'am."

Noya nodded, giving the hunter a distracted wave as she bent to pick up the silver locket from the ground. The hollow hum of pearls rolling across the floor filled the room as she studied it intently, just as Liam had only moments before. "Where did you find this?"

"By the rocks next to the rapids. South of the Castle." Liam explained for the other man. "Just because they found it though, doesn't mean that -"

"Was there anything else?" Noya addressed the hunter directly, cutting her son off mid-sentence. "Any..." Her voice trailed off as if she were afraid that saying the words would make them real.

Jack shook his head. "No, ma'am. But as I was telling young Liam here, there was... well..." He flushed, hesitant to describe the scene again in front of a woman. "It don't look good, Mistress Mercat. It don't look good at all."

Noya glanced at her son, waiting for him to elaborate. He sighed and closed his eyes. "There were blood stains, Mother. A lot of them."

"Oh." She slumped against the wall behind her heavily, as if the floor had given way beneath her feet. The last of the pearls slipped through her fingers, and her other hand flew to her chest. "Oh."

"It might not be anything, Mother." Liam was quick to reassure her. He rushed to her side and guided her to a stool behind the counter. The very same one Letty would sit on when they would watch their father work when they were younger. "Maybe it's from an animal or... or... I don't know. But she could still be alive."

Noya brushed tears from her cheeks. But where he had raged in anger, hers was quiet and still. "No, Liam. No."

"She's strong. She's smart. Grandfather taught her everything - just like he taught me."

"Clearly he didn't teach her enough." Noya whispered. "Or she decided to take matters into her own hands." She continued, giving voice to the family's biggest fear - that Letty might take her own life rather than be married off to a man she didn't care for.

He shook his head. "I don't believe that."

"Liam, please."

"I don't believe any of this! You might be ready to give up, but I'm not! I refuse to accept that she's dead. That she took her own life." His voice grew louder and louder as he continued to speak. So did the pounding in his heart, until it was almost impossible to hear anything that Jack or his mother had to say.

Rather than stay by Noya's side, like he knew a good son should, he strode from the room, his boot heels pounding against the hard-wooden floor. His steps carried him out of the house and across the yard to where his horse was stabled. Before he fully realized what he was doing, the beast was saddled and he was astride it. He urged her out of town, in the direction of the rapids South of the castle. He would find the spot Jack told him about, and he would prove them wrong. He would prove them all wrong.

Chapter Twenty

The next night, Mattie found herself arriving at the house with the chestnut horse a bit earlier than normal.

The village was eerily quiet when she approached it. If it wasn't for the dim glow of candlelight behind tightly drawn curtains, and the soft cry of babies in the night, she might have thought that it was abandoned. After waiting a few moments, she decided to chance it. To her surprise, not even the bully boys were out and about doing their patrols, and she was able to walk straight down the streets, rather than darting from shadow to shadow.

The barn door was already ajar when she got there, and inside she could see that the stall door was also unlatched. She quickly crossed the yard and entered the barn only to find that, yes, her new friend the horse was missing. She frowned to herself; there was no way her friends could have found her hiding spot - they hadn't left the castle since the day they had abandoned her - and she'd always been so careful not to leave any sign of her presence for the Villagers to discover.

Mattie didn't think the beast was dead; it had always appeared in the best of health when she visited it, and she didn't think that it had been claimed by old age. She counted the days on her fingers just to make sure, and, unless she'd lost track of things again, it had only been a month since being locked out of the castle, and only three weeks since she started visiting the horse during her late-night wanderings.

So where was the pretty chestnut then? Her pockets were full of apples for it, and she'd even stolen a couple of choice carrots from the farmer when she passed through his field earlier. She could leave them for it to find, but she worried that its owner might discover them instead and start locking things up at night.

As she debated about what to do, Mattie heard the clatter of iron horse shoes against the hard-packed mud outside the barn. There was no other entrance to the building, and nowhere close by that she could hide – which left the hayloft. She jumped for the ladder that lead to the rafters above. After climbing the rungs two at a time, she hid in the shadows at the top, watching as a young man with red hair led the chestnut into the barn. The very same young man she had run into while scaring the pub goers with Rordan and Talesin. She was also certain she had spied him at the bridge as well. She cursed to herself silently – out of all the horses she decided to make friends with, why did it have to be his?

He tied its bridle to the front of its stall and deftly freed the animal of its saddle. Then he left it in its stall while he carried the saddle towards the back of the barn and disappeared from sight. Mattie stepped onto the ladder, thinking that now would be the best time to make her escape, but the red-haired man quickly reappeared, carrying a bucket full of feed and a large brush.

She cursed again and quickly pulled her foot off the ladder before he could see her. It appeared that she was stuck here until he left, and it didn't look like he intended to leave any time soon. She sighed and pulled her cloak around her, then sat on a hay bale to wait. Hopefully he would leave before dawn, but if he didn't, at least the hay was softer than some other hidey holes she'd spent the day time hours tucked away in.

"Liam? Is that you?" A woman's voice called from outside. Mattie eased further back into the shadows as a matronly woman carrying a lantern entered the barn next. The red-haired man didn't pay any attention to her - instead he started to brush the chestnut down with sharp rough strokes. The horse didn't seem to mind the abuse at all though. In fact, it leaned into it, one lip curling upwards in delight even as its ears flattened at the woman's tone. "Where have you been the past day? The pubs closed for the sabbath over an hour ago."

"I wasn't at the pubs." The man finally answered, but he still didn't look up from his work.

"Then where were you?"

"You know where."

"Liam! You went out there again? You did, didn't you?" The woman's breath hitched. "You promised!"

"I know, but what Jack found changed things."

"Yes, yes it has." The older woman paused, her breath hitching with unshed tears once more. "I know this is hard for you, but it's been over two months. And now, with the necklace... I think it's time to accept that your sister is..."

"Don't say it." He snapped. "They haven't found the body yet - she could still be out there. She could still be alive."

"Two months, Liam."

"Letty's a smart girl."

Mattie frowned. She recognized that name. Hadn't he called her that when she ran into him before? His sister? She leaned forward to hear what they were saying better.

"I know she is, but the blood Jack found."

"I saw what he was talking about. It looked like a stain from a mud puddle to me."

"Liam..." The woman sighed, and her shoulders slumped. "Not even she could survive that long by herself if she was that badly injured."

"She's my sister, I would know if something happened to her."

In the shadows, Mattie stiffened as she realized what she was hearing. A girl from the town went missing two months ago. Two months ago would have been about the time she discovered Marionette in her father's workshop - if her memory could be trusted. Without any coal to mark the walls, she'd given up on keeping track of things. She had even abandoned her nightly mantra. But Marionette's hair was red just like Liam's. Which meant that Marionette must be Letty, his beloved sister. She had suspected it all along – ever since the incident on the bridge – but to finally have it confirmed...

She smothered her groan with her cloak. Out of all the barns in the village, why did she choose to sneak into the one that belonged to the family of the girl who she'd found lying in her father's workshop? The one he turned into a doll? A doll he later gave to the King?

"Has it occurred to you that the blood might not be hers?" Liam asked his mother.

"I prayed that it was someone else's. That she was still alive, but, Jack is right, if she was alive, why hasn't she come home by now?"

"Maybe because she doesn't want to be married off to that troll of a man she's promised to." Liam went back to brushing the horse, violently whisking the dust off its coat.

The woman hissed. "What if one of *them* catches you? Or follows you back home?"

"Them? That's nothing but old wives' tales. It's just a ruined castle, Mother. There's nothing there." Liam sighed. Mattie snorted to herself at that. If only he knew. Down below, Liam stopped brushing the horse long enough to peer up at the hay loft where she was hiding. She scooted farther back into the shadows, and after a minute or two the outsider turned back to his chore. "Nothing's going to happen to me Mother. It's just an old abandoned castle."

"Promise me!" She shouted, startling the horse. It laid its ears back and bared its teeth, shying away from the sudden outburst, and it took several moments before Liam could calm it down. The woman sniffed, and wiped tears from her cheeks. "I won't lose another child."

He stepped out of the stall and pulled her into a hug. "Yes, Mother. I promise."

She patted his cheek. "You're a good boy, Liam. Your father will be proud of you when he finally gets back."

In the dim light, Mattie could see his jaw clench. "Why don't you go back inside? It's cold out here."

The woman murmured something in reply to her son. She turned away, taking the lantern with her as she left the barn. Liam stared after her for a second, and went about bedding the horse down for the night. Once there was fresh bedding under its hooves and feed in its pail, he grabbed a pitchfork off a hook on the wall and approached the ladder with it held in front of him like a weapon. "I know someone's up there." He called out. "Show yourself."

Mattie looked around frantically for a way out but the loft was surrounded on three sides by rough wooden walls. She briefly thought about covering herself up with the hay - there was more than enough lying around - but she wouldn't put it past the man to shove the pitchfork into the piles to make sure no one was hiding in it.

She studied him from her spot in the shadows; he was taller than her by at least a head or two, and much stronger judging by his heavier build. She assumed that he wouldn't be as quick on his feet because of his size, and if he was, her appearance should frighten him away just like she had scared the drunk man outside of the pub. A small thread of doubt made her question her plan though – Liam hadn't run like the drunk man did the first time he saw her. She doubted he would find her terrifying this time either. And didn't he just admit to the old woman that he didn't believe in the Undying Ones?

She didn't have a choice though; it was either hide and wait to be attacked or attack. So, she waited for him to climb up into the hayloft. The moment he stepped away from the ladder, she bolted straight for him, growling like a wild animal.

Mattie saw his blue eyes widen in surprise when she rushed him and heard his muttered oath when he recognized the mask she wore. But just like before, he stood his ground instead of flinching away as others had. He dropped his pitchfork and grabbed her before she could slip past him, swinging her back in the opposite direction. Her mask and bits of hay went flying as she stumbled to the floor, and he leapt on her.

185

She twisted and turned, trying to get free, but he was heavy and he easily pinned her with her arms stretched above her head and his knees on either side of her waist. She bared her teeth in a snarl and glared at him; how dare he trap her so! How dare he make her lose her mask! Surely now that he could see her horrible face he would run away in fear!

But Liam didn't falter - he just raised an eyebrow at her and waited until she stopped growling at him. Finally, he spoke, "Who are you and what are you doing hiding in my barn?"

That, was it? That was all he had to say to her? She stared at him in surprise. "You... you aren't scared of me?"

"Why would I be scared of you? You're a girl. Granted, you're a damned wily one, but I outweigh you by a good couple stones."

"Because I'm a monster! I'm cursed!"

He leaned back, letting go of her wrists, and laughed. Tipped his head back and laughed and laughed and laughed. "Who sent you? Jack? One of the lads at the pub? Did they make you leave that note too? I wouldn't put it past them to have such poor taste - or maybe they haven't heard the news yet."

She shook her head, utterly confused by his behavior. "I don't know what you're talking about."

He jerked his head at the floor of the barn below. "I highly doubt you were sleeping through all that. But if you were, let me fill you in. My sister went missing, and everyone and their mother has been harping on and on about how it must have been one of them that took her. The monsters that lurk about in the forest at night time."

"It's true."

"No, it's not."

She licked her lips. "But it is. Can't you see? I was deformed by the plague."

Again, the sharp laughter burst past his lips. "There hasn't been a plague in over a hundred years! You look perfectly normal to me; in fact, you might even be pretty...once you take a bath."

Mattie froze. What did he say? She was... normal looking? Pretty even? Was he blind? Or had grief driven him mad?

Liam nodded at where her mask rested a short distance away. "I've seen you before, haven't I? The night little Johanna saw the phantoms in her yard? You ran into me on Market Street."

"I don't know what you're talking about."

"Sure, you do. You're probably the one Will Barbs says he saw outside the Prancing Bulldog too."

"The prancing what?" Bulldogs didn't prance! In her short experience with them, they either growled at you and tried to bite you, or slobbered on you and barked when you left.

"Bulldog - the pub on High street. Or maybe you're one of the ones that like to stalk the Rusty Shoe."

She didn't answer him. Instead she tried to twist around underneath him again, straining to reach her mask. Even if she was 'normal' looking her face felt naked without his comforting weight. She was able to brush the mask with her fingertips and knock it closer until she could grab it. She quickly pulled it back over her face, blocking her supposed beauty from his sight.

His eyes flicked over her face. "Yes, you're definitely the one."

"How would you know? You were drunk!"

"Ha! You admit it!"

Mattie glared at him and crossed her arms over her chest. "How do you remember any of that?"

"You kicked me in the balls, hit me with a bag full of bread, and called me an oaf." Liam said. "You made quite the impression."

"Hmf."

"Now, who are you? And what are you doing in my barn? Are you one of those thieves who's been going around stealing food? You won't find any here."

"I wasn't looking for food…"

"Then what were you going to do? Steal a horse?"

"What would I do with a horse?"

"I'm not the thief, so why don't you tell me."

She continued to glare at him, and found herself grinding her teeth together too. If all villagers were this infuriating, then she was glad they were locked out of the castle. "I am not a thief."

He cocked his head to one side, staring down at her through his eyelashes.

"Liam? Are you still out there? Who are you talking to?" His mother's voice called out, and they both turned to watch the circle of light from her lantern grown closer to the barn door.

Mattie sent a silent thank you to whatever god cared about her enough to provide her with a distraction whenever she needed to escape. She sat up, trying to drive her head into his chin, but he dodged it and pushed her back down.

"Nothing, Mother." He called out. His use of force knocked her mask askew again so that she could only see out of one eye. She felt him press his hand against her lips, silencing her. "Don't say a word unless you want her to call the bailiff." He hissed softly.

Mattie didn't want to find out what a bailiff was, but she also didn't want to stay here and let Liam interrogate her any more. Since there was no way she could escape from her position underneath him, she did the only thing she could think of - she bit him.

It was a small bite, hardly worse than one might get if they were nipped by a naughty dog, but it was hard enough to draw a little blood. She could feel it trickling over her lips and taste the smallest drop of metallic bitterness on her tongue. It was thicker than water, warm, and sweeter than any wine she could ever imagine. It made her feel strange, as if she was buzzing with energy and seeing clearly for the first time. She could sense more of it pulsing through Liam's body. Through his heart and under his skin. The urge to push him over and tear it out was overwhelming, and terrifying. She ached to drink him dry and strip his flesh from his bones until there was nothing left of him.

Liam yelped and he pulled his hand away from her mouth to inspect the damage. "You bit me! Why did you do that?!" He looked down to glare at her and froze when he saw the look in her eye. "What is wrong with you?"

"Hm?" Her desire to run away from him was suddenly forgotten, drifting away like so mist in the morning sun. She wanted to taste more of him. Now. She reached up to grab his hand, to pull it back to her mouth. How strange, she thought, as soon as her hand touched his, she could feel his muscles tense and his heart start to race in his chest.

"Hey! Stop that!" He jerked away, quickly crawling off her and backing away until several feet separated them. He crouched in the corner, his injured hand cradled against his chest while he searched for the pitchfork with the other.

When Mattie drew closer her vision started to swim and shift until it wasn't Liam hiding from her. A lanky man with dark hair cowered corner lined damp stone and not rough wood. "Stay away from me, demon!" he cried out.

The words reverberated in her head, disorienting her even further. His accent was familiar; thick and heavy, with rolling 'r's. She longed to hear more of it, but the man kept shouting hateful words at her, each one making her heart break a little more.

Dybbuk.

Vampyr.

Ghoul.

Revenant.

And on and on and on.

She pressed her hands against her ears to block it out. "Stop!" Curling in on herself. "Stop it now!"

The voice in her head rose to a sharp crescendo and then suddenly fell silent at her command. She opened her eyes to find that the space around her turned back into the hayloft again. The walls were wooden once more, and the straw underneath her feet was fresh. Down below she could see the pretty chestnut horse munching on it's feed. A hand touched her shoulder, surprising her. Instinctively she shoved its owner away, and there was a thud as a body hit the wall. Mattie stared at the limp form of Liam and then at her hands in amazement. Where did the strength to do that come from?

And then she remembered the taste of Liam's blood and the sensation of power crawling through her veins like lightening. Had that little taste given her this ability?

The body shifted again until it was no longer Liam lying there - instead the lanky man with the dark hair replaced him once more. But now he was covered in gore; his stomach was ripped open and bite marks lined his intestines. Skin and muscle was missing from his arms and legs and neck. His eyes were closed and he was struggling to breathe, little bubbles of blood appearing at the corners of his mouth with each laborious rise of his chest. "What have you done dear one?" He asked, his eyes glazing over with pain as he prepared to leave this world for the next. "What has he turned you into?"

Mattie scrambled backwards as the body rose, the horrible mess of skin and torn muscle melting away until it was just Liam again. He was frowning at her again - however, this time it was more out of surprise than anger. "How did you...?"

"Stay away from me!"

He dropped the pitchfork and held out his hands to his sides. "I'm not going to hurt you..."

"Leave me alone!" Her hands found the top of the ladder and she half slid, half fell down it. She ignored his shouts to stop and rushed out the barn door, past the old woman in the night gown, and into the cool night air.

Chapter Twenty-One

Mattie ran.

She zigged and zagged through the streets of the village and then through the fields of crops around the farms. She could hear men chasing her. The hooves of their horses pounding the ground behind her, could feel their dogs snapping at her heels - but when she looked behind, no one was there. Ahead of her the world continued to twist and turn and tilt; one moment she was surrounded by tall stalks of wheat, the next she saw castle walls. First Liam called after her, then the dark-haired man from her vision, and then she heard the King's voice, and her father's.

She clasped her hands against her ears, demanding that they be silent. Ordering them to leave her alone. But they kept harassing her, until their voices drowned out the noise of the invisible hounds and horses.

The fields stopped abruptly and the forest began right at their edge. She hopped the low fence designed to keep deer and other creatures out and plunged on blindly into the night. She dodged trees and jumped over rocks. She kept running, forcing one foot to land after the other, even though her sides burned and she was gasping for breath.

No matter what she did, no matter where she turned, they were there; the hounds and the horses, the men and the King. Rordan and Talesin. Father and Liam. They yelled and shouted names at her as they hunted her. First, they called her demon, then dybbuk, then cannibal, vampyr, flesh eater, and witch.

Finally, she could go no further and she fell to her knees, completely spent and exhausted. She pressed her hands against her ears. "Stop! Please stop!"

The voices continued their assault. She screamed at them until her throat was raw, but their volume continued to rise until it was all she could hear.

She felt a crack as something collided with the back of her head, and then there was finally silence.

A man dressed in shadows stood at the end of the bed. The lady assumed he was Death finally coming to take her away, but when he spoke she realized that she was not so lucky – it was only him, the one who had sent the old woman to her rooms and cursed her to this half-life.

"She's dead." He announced after surveying her for some time.

The lady wanted to laugh. Of course she was dead, she couldn't breathe and her heart no longer beat in her chest. She lay on the bed, perfectly still and as cold as ice, and had been so for hours.

But she wasn't free yet – her eyes could still see and she had had to watch, unable to cry out, as the woman had made her way around the room stealing everything and anything valuable and small enough to fit in her pockets.

"No, she still lives, she still breathes." The old woman insisted from nearby.

The man walked to the side of the bed, and the shadows fell away to reveal his handsome face. He pressed his fingers against the lady's throat. "I do not feel her heart beating." He moved his hand so that it hovered over her nose and mouth. "I do not feel her breathing."

He might not be able to feel any life in her body, but, oh, how she could feel the life in his. The heat radiating from his hand was so warm it could burn her skin, and his heartbeat was steady and strong. And even though she could not breathe, she could still smell him somehow. His scent drifted into her nose. If she were still alive, if she could still move, she imagined her nose would twitch at how... good... he smelled. Better than good; he smelled like sunshine, and the forest that surrounded the castle. Like the finest mulled wine on a cold winter's night.

Her mouth began to water, and a strange hunger made her stomach cramp. Her desire to feast on him, to drink his blood, to take his warmth and life from him was so strong that it surprised her.

It wasn't possible - was it? She was dead. She shouldn't feel these things. She shouldn't feel anything at all. And why would she want to eat him like he was a trussed-up pig? Men and women did not eat each other for sustenance. God had created animals for that purpose.

But the hunger inside of her was building until all she could focus on was the beating of his heart and the blood pulsing through his veins.

"There!" The old woman cried out, rushing into the lady's field of vision. "She moved!"

He glared at her. "Are you mad? She's dead. She can't move."

The old woman ignored him, and continued to point at the lady. "I'm not mad. She is alive. See, she's breathing!"

The old woman was right, the lady realized with a start – she was breathing again. The air inside of the room was stuffy from the windows and door being closed for so long, but she could breathe without any pain or coughing. She closed her eyes and inhaled slowly, savoring the sensation - and the delicious scent of the man standing by the bed.

"You're..." Whatever the man was about to say died on his lips. "Her eyes are closed now."

"See!" The old woman cackled.

His scent grew more intense as he held his hand back over her nose and lips. "She's breathing. She wasn't breathing before." He grabbed her hand off the bed and squeezed it. "My la..."

The lady opened her eyes and glared at him. How dare he try to use endearments with her? She no longer felt afraid of the hunger growing inside of her; after everything he had done to her, it was only fitting that she consume him and use his life to free her from this place. His touch made her skin crawl, but she tightened her hand around his and pulled him closer. He continued to stare at her in wonder.

"Shall we get you something to eat, dearie? A nice thick stew? Maybe a shepherd's pie? You've been out for quite a while..." The old woman rambled on, a worried expression on her face. She began slowly edging towards the door.

He, however, was oblivious to the danger he was in. He allowed her to pull him closer, his light blue eyes studying her features intently. He ran the fingers of his free hand over her cheeks and neck, "You're barely even *scarred. Woman, you have worked a miracle. We'll need more of that potion of yours – it'll have to be distributed to the guards first..."*

He did not get a chance to finish his instructions, for the Lady attacked.

Chapter Twenty~Two

Mattie was floating.

Her consciousness was struggling to surface in the muddy mess that was her brain, but it kept being dragged back down into the darkness. She caught glimpses of shadowy tree branches from between her eyelashes, only to fall back into visions of that horrible sick room again. The next time she found the strength open her eyes again, she saw the night sky above her.

There was a weird pounding in her left ear; a thumpthump, thumpthump, thumpthump, interwoven with a wheezing rattle. She tried to bat it, whatever it was, away, but the noise was persistent.

"Hey, stop that." A familiar voice commanded. "You're hard enough to carry as it is without you fighting me."

It was then that she realized that she wasn't floating - she was being carried.

Her bare cheek was pressed against soft short hair, her arms loosely swinging back and forth with every step. A knee bumped against her chest, and something hard and curved dug into her belly. She opened her eyes and caught a glimpse of chestnut hide, gleaming in golden light. She looked up and saw the sun shining down through the trees. It turned the leaves overhead nearly translucent, and washed the earth in bright polka dots.

In the back of her mind, she knew she should be afraid of it, that she should not be out in it, but it was hard to stay focused and alert. Her head was throbbing, and the gentle movement of the horse underneath her was rocking her back to sleep even though she had been thrown across it rather haphazardly.

Content that she was not dying like she had thought – which was silly, because how could someone who was already dead die again? - and that the voices were finally silent, Mattie let the darkness take her once more and fell asleep.

The next time Mattie woke, the sun was still out. It shined through a window on the wall opposite the bed she was laying in. Even though the curtains hanging in front of it had been closed, its rays still leached through and made her eyes sting. She blinked rapidly against the glare and turned her head away, but despite the pain, she found herself drawn back to it, over and over and over again.

Sunlight. She couldn't remember the last time she had actually seen proper sunlight.

And stranger still, she couldn't remember the last time she had ever been out in it.

She inspected her hands, expecting to find them covered in welts and scorch marks, but they were clean. She ran her fingertips over her face, and was shocked to discover that it, too, was free of any damage. How was that possible? Perhaps her clothing and her mask had protected her?

Remembering her mask, Mattie's hands flew back up to her face. It was naked, free for the world to see. She sat up, searching for it amongst the bedclothes, but it wasn't there. A quick glance around the room she was in revealed that it was sitting on a dresser next to the window - along with the rest of her clothes. Then what was she wearing? She flung back the thick blankets to find that she had been changed into a nightgown similar to the one the old woman had been wearing the night before. The fabric was finer than anything she had ever felt before, thin and soft, and pure white. She doubted she had ever worn anything so nice. Not even in the dreams that plagued her.

The sheets and quilt on the bed were equally luxurious, and the mattress... oh the mattress. She didn't think she could ever go back to sleeping on rocks and dirt after sleeping on a proper bed. But she must at some point, she couldn't really stay here, wherever here was.

She swung her legs over the side of the bed, and they were met by a carpet that was just as thick as the mattress. She sighed as her feet sank into the soft nap. This must be how kings and queens live.

After a moment of relishing in her surroundings, Mattie forced herself to leave the safety of the bed and crossed the smooth hardwood floor to the dresser. The sun was brighter here, and its rays touched her toes. She jerked her foot back, hissing in anticipation, but nothing happened.

Odd.

She stuck her toes back into the sunlight and left it there, waiting. The sun is warm, hot even, but she didn't burn at its touch. No smoke rose from her skin, nor did it crack under the assault. She wiggled her toes, then put her whole foot into the sunlight, then her leg, and her arm. Finally, she reached out and pushed back the curtains until she was completely bathed in warm light.

Mattie giggled, twirling so she could feel the warmth of the sun all over her body. Dust motes swirled around her, gleaming in the bright light and dancing with her. How, she wondered, could she had ever been afraid of this?

Someone cleared his throat interrupting her moment of joy. She stopped abruptly, looking over her shoulder to find Liam watching her from the doorway. He leaned one shoulder against the jamb, his arms crossed over his chest. "Welcome back to the world of the living. I was starting to wonder when you might wake up."

"You... you're the one who brought me here?" She was surprised that a villager would show her any kindness. Especially after everything she had taken from them over the past month.

"Yes." He scratched at his neck. "Well, mother insisted."

She flushed. "Thank you."

"Thank her, when she sees you."

"I thought she was going to call the bailiff on me."

"She was set to, but she changed her mind." He cocked his head, listening for something she couldn't hear yet. "It helped that I lied and told her that you were Old Marley's Granddaughter come to see him."

Mattie stared at him in shock. "What?"

"I told her that the boy who was hiding in our barn got away. You are Marley's Granddaughter come to visit him. You were out late on the road at night because you thought Mill-On-Rye was closer to your homestead than it actually is. You were accosted by ruffians, and I saved you."

"I don't know who this... Marley is." It felt as if the world was tilting under her feet again, and the room swam before her eyes, momentarily replaced by stone walls and damp floors.

Rordan squatted before her, his brother and the stranger from the dungeon watching from a short distance away. "The Toymaker is your father..."

"He's an old man in the village. Strange, like you. I'll introduce you to him later today." Liam spoke, bringing her back to the present. "After I've had a chance to speak to him about this charade. Now are you with me? Or would you rather spend the night in the town goal?"

Mattie stared at him, frowning as she considered her options. Either she could lie, as he clearly wanted her to, and continue to live in luxury, or be locked up in a cell – which was probably as comfortable as her cave. While she had slept in far worse places, she was loathe to leave the soft mattress and clean clothes just yet. "One question first."

"Fair enough, but quickly now. She'll be up here any moment."

"Why?"

"Why?"

"Yes. Why lie for me? You don't know me. All I've done is cause you and your town nothing but trouble."

"Well, maybe by taking you in, I'll be doing you and the town a favor. Since you'll be provided for, hopefully you'll stop your thieving ways and leave the poor bairns alone." He continued to linger in the doorway, studying her as if she were some strange artifact. There was more that he wanted to say, she could feel it lingering on the air alongside the after effects of her vision.

"And?"

"You mentioned the castle last night. You've been in there, haven't you?"

He wanted her to take him to his sister. She shook her head, knowing that he wouldn't like what he would find. If there was anything left to find. "No, there isn't."

Liam snarled. "Lies. Keep it up and I really will go get the bailiff."

For a moment, Mattie considered playing meek like she did for the King. But then she realized that his bark was no worse than Rordan's or Talesin's, or even her father's. Plus, she had just as much power over him as he did over her. "And what will they do to you if they find out you've been harboring a thief? Throw you in the stocks? I'm sure your family will appreciate that after what your sister has put them through."

His eyes flashed, and he took a step forward. However, the sound of footsteps coming up the stairs stopped him. He glanced behind him. "She's coming. Mind your manners."

"Excuse me?"

"No biting." Liam held up his hand to show her the bandage wrapped around it. She could see faint lines starting to sneak across his skin from underneath the plain linen. "It's been two days and it still bloody hurts."

She flushed, remembering the power that had coursed through her veins at the taste of his flesh. The hunger rose in her throat once more, but she bit her cheek rather than give in to it. Her own blood was bitter and bland compared to his. "I'm sorry."

"Help me find my sister, and all will be forgiven."

Mattie opened her mouth to reply, but her words died on her lips as the matronly woman from the night before stepped into the doorway. She paused, her eyes darting from Mattie to Liam and back again. "I thought I heard talking."

Liam crossed his arms over his chest again. "I was walking past when I saw that our guest was awake. I was just checking in on her to see if she needed anything."

"Hmf." The woman seemed appeased by his answer. "What she probably needs is for you to tell her Grandfather that she's here."

"Yes, Mother." He turned to leave the room, but he was stopped by her hand grabbing his arm.

"Introduce us first.

"Hm?"

"Our house may be in chaos, but we won't forget our manners."

Liam sighed, "Yes, Mother. Miss Marley, this is my Mother, Noya Mercat." He gestured loosely at the woman next to him. "Mother, this is Miss Marley..."

Mattie wrinkled her nose at all the 'M's. While it would make things easier to remember, it was quite a mouthful. She gave the woman her best curtsey - it was more than a little sloppy, it being many centuries since she had last used it – and when she spoke, she tried her best to mimic the speech of the heroines from the books in the library.

"It's Mattie, ma'am. Mattie Framer." The lies spilled from her lips easily, even though the disorientation had returned and threatened to overwhelm her. She stood back up slowly and forced herself to smile. "Thank you, and your son, for all your assistance."

Enjoy this preview of the next book in
The Undying Ones!
Elusion
Out this Spring!

Elusion

Mattie studied the miniature that Marley had handed her. It was of a man with dark hair and bright eyes, but even though it was rough and primitive, something about it bothered her. "Who is this?"

"My many times great grandfather."

"Oh." That must be it then. She could see the family resemblance in the bright eyes and hooked nose.

"He was a toymaker – a useless trade, back in those days. But he used to be capable of making such intricate little things. I still have one of his creations in the attic. Somehow, Lord knows how, it's survived all these centuries."

"My father is a toymaker."

Marley smiled at her. "I'm going to guess, based on how young Liam found you, that it's still a useless trade."

"You could say that." She forced herself to return his smile and passed the miniature back to him. "What happened to him?"

"I imagine he died, either from old age, or from the plague." Instead of taking it away, he wrapped her fingers around it and stood. "The story goes that he was a particular favorite of the Queen."

"Oh?" Mattie felt her mouth dry and her blood run cold at his words.

"He was madly in love with her, and supposedly she was in love with him too. When the Black Death came, he abandoned his family and went to her. He was locked inside with the rest of them, and I suppose, his bones are still rattling around up there."

She glanced down at the miniature in her hand. "Yes, I suppose they are."

About the Author

Christina Olson has been writing stories since she was very little and once got in trouble for insisting that 'are' was actually spelled 'ar'. Thankfully she's since learned the error of her ways, and now spends her days toiling away on her many projects. When she isn't chained to her computer, she enjoys chasing her son around and spending time with her husband.

Made in the USA
Lexington, KY
05 September 2017